the way back

Tom Pawlik

Visit Tom Pawlik's website at www.tompawlik.com

The Way Back.

Published by Mo Dog Media

Scripture quotations from *The Holy Bible* King James Version.

ACKNLOWLEDGMENTS:

To my beloved Colette: lover, friend, wife, and mother of my children. I love you more than I have space to write. Thank you for your constant encouragement, and your steadfast love, and for making our home a place I love to be. *Many women do noble things, but you surpass them all. Prov 31:29*

To my dear children: Andrew, Aryn, Jordan, John, Jessi, and Alexa. I love you each more than you will ever know. Thank you for filling our home with the sweet noise of life.

FOREWORD

The Little Novel That Could.

This novel was conceived and born a humble short story in 1993 as part of a college writing class. It was one of those exceptional stories that just seem to write themselves. And when complete, it immediately took a special place in my heart.

But alas, in those days a short story would rarely find its way to publication. One might say it was easier for a camel to pass through the eye of a needle.

So the little story waited patiently. And as it waited, it began to grow and mature. It grew stronger and broader in scope, and its voice began to change. And after a few years, it came into its own as the humble little novel you see today.

It was read by publishers who said some very nice things about it, all while declining to publish it. It even took 2nd place in the first Operation First Novel Contest run by the Christian Writer's Guild. The very same contest I would go on to win two years later with *Vanish.*

So the little novel continued to wait patiently even while four of its younger siblings found their way to print ahead of it.

One of the reasons it never found a home with a traditional publisher may have been that its genre was a little hard to classify. It is a coming of age tale. It is an adventure with plenty of suspense. And I think it may even be southern fiction—a genre I never knew existed.

In short, it is heart wrenching, heart warming, and heart pounding.

But however you wish to categorize it, I want you to know that I believe in this novel whole-heartedly. It is still my favorite. And having just gone through a final bit of trimming and grooming, I find I love it even more these twenty years since it was born.

So now, thanks to the numerous advancements in technology like laptops and smart phones and Kindles and iPads and Nooks and crannies and Al Gore's Internet, our little novel is finally ready to step out into the sun.

I hope you enjoy it as much as I do.

For Aryn, my storyteller.

1

Mississippi, 1978

His name was Abraham. He had lived in a shack at the edge of the swamp for as long as I could remember. Everything I knew of him before that summer ten years ago had come mostly from rumors and hearsay. Folks in Silas don't have much else to occupy their time so it's not surprising there were so many stories about the man.

Today there are even more.

I stood in the doorway of his darkened room and my heart nearly broke at the sight of him. I remembered Abe Garner as tall and powerful, barrel-chested with strong arms and thick hands. Though I never knew his exact age, and though the sun had creased his coffee-colored skin like old leather, I hadn't really thought of him before as being *old*. But here, now, he looked to me so frail and small.

Pencil-thin rays of sunlight streamed through the blinds and draped soft amber stripes across his bed. He lay there, obscured in shadows, and I couldn't even make out the features of his face. The room held a musty warmth, as though Abe had brought with him the smell of the swamp to contend against the sterile *un*scent of the Chase County Home for the Elderly.

There was nothing more they could do for him, so they had brought him here to die. He lay so still I thought at first he was already gone. Then I noticed a slight movement under the bedsheet. The light rustle of linen gave way to a faint whisper.

"Paul?"

His voice was so soft, I didn't recognize it at first. I took a step into the room.

"No, it's me, Jake. Jake Kelly."

For a long while there was no answer. I took another step and peered more closely. His eyes glistened in the shadows, gazing back at me like a melancholy hound's.

"Jacob," he said at last. "That you?"

I smiled, relieved that he still knew me, and drew up a chair to his bedside. "Yes sir."

His countenance glowed faintly with a weak grin. "Good to see you again. Been more'n a year since you was in t-town last." His voice wheezed and crackled.

I nodded. "It's been hard to find the time."

College had kept me pretty busy the last four years and too broke to do anything but work over the summers. I hadn't been home since Christmas of my junior year. Frankly, there wasn't much left in Silas to bring me back. And were it not for my sister and mother—and her recent message—I might not have returned at all.

I leaned closer. "Ma called to say you took sick and I should come home right away. She said you wanted to see me."

Abe nodded and motioned to the narrow closet across the room. "I g-got something for you."

I went and retrieved a paper sack from atop a pair of faded leather boots. When I opened the bag, a wave of earthy odors washed over me. My eyes closed as a flood of memories rushed into my head. The rich scent of cattails and juniper mingled with the musty aroma of a tiny shack: mud-stained, cedar floorboards, the sharp, mothball-sting of old clothing, the bite of buckshot and gunpowder. And the faintest trace—almost entirely hidden beneath the others, as if trying not to be noticed but undeniably there…

The pungent scent of a wet hound.

My eyes snapped open and I looked at the object in my hands. A tattered, leather-bound Bible, as creased and worn-out as old Abe himself. I sat down and flipped through the yellowed pages. The print was barely readable but I could make out the faded scrawl of handwritten notes in the margins of almost every page. The book felt thick and heavy in my hands, yet at the same time it seemed so delicate and frail.

"It's the only thing of value I still own," Abe said. "I wanted to g-give it to somebody who'd see that it got put to g-good use."

I looked back at Abe, not sure of what to say. "I'll try."

"See that you do, boy." Abe closed his eyes and breathed a deep sigh, as though he had finally completed some great task and now was at peace. "Set here a while with me, will you?"

We sat for a long time in silence and soon he drifted into sleep. I paged through the old Bible and moved my chair closer to the window. Opening the blinds a bit more, I began to read some of the notes Abe had written in the margins. Mostly, they consisted of his thoughts and comments on whatever passage he had been reading. There were also a few of his own brief prayers written out as well. Things like: *Lord, help me not to be hateful or spiteful*, or *Keep me from saying things out of meanness*.

Nearly every page had something underlined or commented on in some way, and as I read through them I found myself shaking my head. Folks in Silas would have been genuinely surprised to learn that Abe Garner even knew how to read and write. Most people considered him a senile old hermit. A few thought he was just a poor and lonely old man, while fewer still knew the kind of man he truly was. Usually, we make up our minds about people without taking the time to learn the truth. Soon, we begin to believe those things without much regard as to whether or not they are true. Such was the case, I must admit, for myself until I had come to know Abraham Garner that June when I was twelve.

2

Summer had settled over our community that year with a vengeance, smothering it like a heavy wool blanket. The air felt thick with humidity and the sun hammered down relentlessly most days, sparing us only briefly during occasional fits of downpours.

Silas itself is tucked away on a patch of Route 47 where it crosses the Shawno River. It's barely a dot on most maps. In fact, it's a popular saying here that if you ever get lost while traveling in Mississippi, and you find yourself at some point farthest away from any big city or major highway, then stop in for a visit because your probably right near Silas.

Thirty years ago, Cyrus Meade had donated some land to the town. The Meades were the richest family in the whole county. Cyrus owned quite a bit of land, and a bank or two, and even the newspaper up in Chase. The land he donated was right along the river just outside of Silas. The town council had voted to use it for a park where folks could go for picnics and such. Shortly afterward, they started having a summer festival there on the weekend right after school let out. Over the years, it had grown into quite an event, with contests and craft shows, and even a Ferris wheel they'd bring down all the way from Chase. It would last the entire weekend and close with a pig roast and fireworks on Sunday night. My father would often chuckle at the whole affair saying, "Yessir, a regular slice of Americana."

That may have been true, but as kids, we looked forward to that event more than anything. It was our way of celebrating the end of the school year, and I can remember sitting in class that last day, feeling giddy as we listened to the distant pounding and sawing of carnival booths under construction. Then came the throaty growl of the semi-truck as it pulled the Ferris wheel into town. It seemed to take forever for that last bell to ring, but when it finally did, we knew the school year was over and the summer vacation we had yearned for since September had arrived at last.

There was a certain ritual I followed on my way home each day. I would cut across the field behind the school, weave through a patch of bushes, and emerge onto the main street that ran through town. I followed it past the hardware store, the barber shop, the florist, and the bank until I finally reached my favorite spot in town: Buckman's Drugstore.

Now it was no secret that Mrs. Buckman could make the finest rootbeer floats in the whole county, so Buckman's was always a popular place. It seemed everyone in town stopped by at least once during the day, and some came in quite a bit more. Most afternoons, the place was occupied by four old men in particular. They came to share war stories and such, and to keep each other company so as to remind themselves that the world hadn't passed them by and left them forgotten.

Mort Krasky and Jolly Meyer would commandeer one of the four booths in the front of the store for a game of chess. Yancey Buckman would give advice from a stool at the counter. And Clem Anderson could always be found standing near the doorway, leaning on his cane and watching the rest of the world outside.

"Hi, Mr. Anderson," I said, as I breezed in through the door.

"Mmhmmm," he mumbled, not even looking down at me.

Old Clem was exceptionally thin and pale, with gray strands of hair combed back across his scalp, and black eyebrows jutting out like a row of tangled shrubbery. And his long, hooked beak of a nose overshadowed a tiny, puckered mouth.

Red, round-faced Jolly Meyer glanced up from his game and grinned. "Don't tell me it's three o'clock already!" He shook his head and his crescent-shaped eyes gleamed. "My how time flies when you're winnin', don't you think Mort?"

"Acchh—just make your move!" Mort Krasky scowled. He seemed lost in thought, staring at his fancy wooden chess pieces through the spectacles perched at the end of his nose. While Jolly's girth filled his side of the booth entirely, Mort had to scoot himself to the edge of his seat just to keep his feet touching the floor.

Yancey Buckman watched the game from his stool at the counter. His tanned face had deep lines and creases, but his dyed-black hair was still thick and wavy. He smiled at me.

"Whatchya say there, Jake?"

I hopped onto the stool next to him. "I say I'd like a rootbeer float to celebrate the last day of school!"

Yancey shook his head. "Well, Mrs. Buckman's gone across the street to get a few things at the grocery. She oughta be back shortly—unless you want *me* to fix you up one of my famous chocolate malt—"

"No thanks," I said, quickly. "I'll wait."

Yancey chuckled and turned back to the game.

I spun around on my stool and watched Clem Anderson watch the rest of the world—or at least the tiny part of it he could see from his place in the doorway. He had hurt his leg in the first World War and so had to use a cane just to get about, which was probably why he was so sour all the time. He owned a locksmith shop in town for many years until he retired, selling it to his son-in-law. He was a widower who now lived alone, and what he did with his time those days, I never knew. Old Clem stood with his nose to the screen, staring out at the empty street. After a few moments, his eyebrows furrowed and his head perked forward like a cat that had just spotted a bird outside its window.

He nodded to himself and grunted. "Well, look who's in town again." He threw a glance backward. "*Abe Garner*."

I hadn't known Abe at that time. I had only seen him occasionally whenever he'd come into town for groceries and such. I never spoke to him directly, although I'd heard just about every rumor there was about him: he lived in the swamp, he ate snakes, he was a murderer hiding from the authorities, he was an eccentric millionaire, he was penniless hermit, he was a witch-doctor, he was a cannibal, he was a ghost.

Mort and Jolly were busy with their game while Yancey looked on. They seemed content to ignore Clem altogether.

Clem shook his head and clicked his tongue. "Looks like he's goin' to the grocery store."

At that, Yancey got up and went over to the big front window. He stood there with his hands shoved into his pockets, jingling his keys softly. I climbed down off my stool for a better view.

Across the street, I spotted a large man in faded overalls and straw hat walking down the sidewalk in front of the grocery store. He was tall, probably even taller than Clem himself. The brim of his hat was tipped low so I couldn't get a good look at his face.

Just as he got to the store entrance, who should come bustling out but Mrs. Buckman herself. She backed out of the door, pushing it open with her hip, and when she spun around, she nearly ran *smack* into old Abe!

At first, she had that surprised look that folks get whenever they bump into someone unexpectedly. She started to smile but quickly realized that the person she had just bumped into wasn't anyone she had ever expected to bump into in the first place. As she looked up, her smile turned back into a look of surprise that grew even more surprised-looking the farther up she looked. But old Abe just tugged off his hat and clutched it to his chest as he held the door open for her. His hair was cotton white and he nodded politely. Mrs. Buckman offered up a nervous smile and then scurried off across the street toward us.

Yancey sighed and returned to his stool.

Clem started chuckling to himself and turned back to the others. "P-p-p-pardon me," he said, imitating the way Abe talked. "B-b-b-but could you sp-p-p-pare any ch-ch-ch-change?"

Mort and Jolly looked up from their game and laughed.

"Now Clem," Jolly said. "You keep makin' fun of him, and pretty soon you're gonna start talkin' like'at yourself."

Yancey shook his head. "He's just a poor old fella. Why can't folks leave him be?"

"Poor old fella?" Clem adjusted his glasses and stared at Yancey. "*Poor old fella*? Why, you don't even know anything about him, do ya? Y'ain't even been livin' in Silas but fifteen years—"

"Clem," Mort said, turning back to his game. "Don't go gittin' yourself all riled up."

"—move down from Chase and open your fancy store," Clem said, without missing a beat. "You don't even know the *real* reason he's been livin' out in that swamp, do you?"

"*Clem*!" Mort turned around in his booth and shot Clem a stern look over his glasses.

Clem glared back at Mort, then he glanced down at me, and his tiny mouth puckered up even tighter. I realized I had been standing there, staring at them with my mouth open.

I wanted to ask Clem what he had meant by his comment, but just then Mrs. Buckman breezed through the door. She was a plump, fair-skinned woman with her gray hair all up in a bun, and her arms loaded with two bags of groceries. She was talking up a storm as she entered.

"…so hot you could bake a cake right on the sidewa—well my goodness, Jacob Kelly, is it that time already? And here it is, the last day of school and I'm out shopping, no thought for how late it's getting—Yancey dear, grab this bag it's slipping—you two still playin' that silly game? You'd think grown men could find a better use of their remaining years than that—oh, I've got to make Jacob his rootbeer float…" She disappeared into the back room, still talking.

Yancey set the grocery bags on the counter. "All I'm saying is that you're not setting a very good example."

"Aww!" Clem waved off the comment.

"He's right, Clem," Mort said. "It ain't a good example for young Jake here."

"Now don't you start in too." Clem wagged a knobby finger at Mort. "You ain't got much use for them folks neither—so don't start judgin' me!"

"I ain't judging you. I'm just sayin' it ain't a very good example is all."

"Aww!"

By then I couldn't contain myself any longer.

"What real reason?"

They all turned to stare at me.

"Why *is* he living all alone out in the swamp?"

Yancey smiled down at me, but his eyes looked kind of sad. "Oh, it's just a lot of nonsense is all. Let's just say that folks around here like to…" he seemed to search for the right word. "…exaggerate things a bit."

With that, old Clem snorted and stormed out.

By that time I was more confused then ever, but just then Mrs. Buckman came out from the back room, tying an apron around her waist, and set about making for me the grandest rootbeer float I had ever had. I sipped it slowly, savoring every mouthful and soon I had forgotten all about old Abe Garner and the swamp.

For the time being.

3

Afterward, I continued home, following the main street out of town. Just across the bridge, I turned right onto Dunworthy Lane, a dusty, gravel road that led for a mile or so down through a wooded hollow and back up a short hill. At the top of the hill stood our big white clapboard farmhouse.

We didn't own a great deal of land, just a dozen acres that we rented out to the neighboring farmers. We had a small barn where we kept a horse, two goats and a few chickens. We weren't farmers in any true sense of the word, although Ma had a big garden behind the house, and there were always enough chores to keep me and my little sister busy.

Pa worked at the paper mill up in Chase, about ten miles north of Silas. They chose to settle here because Pa preferred the country surroundings, even though Chase is hardly what you would call a big city.

I stopped at the mailbox and pulled out a flier for the Summer Festival. They would always print up an advertisement to tell the different events of the carnival, but this year something unusual struck my curiosity:

The Silas Township
Summer Festival Presents:
GATORWORLD'S TRAVELING
REPTILE EXHIBIT
Live Alligators! Live Snakes!
Reptiles from around the world!
Saturday, June 5th at Shawno Park
Children under 13 must be attended
by an adult.

At the time, I'd had the same fascination with alligators that most boys had. There were plenty of them living in the rivers and swamps around Chase County. Warning signs were posted at nearly every beach and boat landing.

The flier listed a number of other contests and exhibits, but this one was clearly the main attraction. For me at least.

I sprinted up the driveway and burst through the screen door into the kitchen. Ma looked up from her cucumber-peeling and raised an eyebrow at me. Her long, blond hair was tied back under a bandana, but a few strands always hung down over her blue eyes, and she was constantly puffing them out of her way. She rubbed her forehead with the back of her wrist.

"You wanna leave the door on its hinges next time, young man?"

"Sorry," I huffed, and slapped the paper down in the only clear spot on the table. "They're having an alligator exhibit at the carnival tomorrow! *Live* alligators!"

Ma's eyebrow remained raised as she glanced down at the flier. "Hmm," she said, "we'll see."

"*We'll see*?" I gaped at her. "Whaddaya mean?"

She curled up the corner of her mouth. "It says children under thirteen need to be accompanied by an adult. As I recall, you're still twelve, yes?"

I frowned, grabbed back the paper, and read the fine print. "Well, no big deal. I figured we'd all go anyway."

She nodded. "We'll see."

Just then, the screen door shot open and my five-year-old sister Molly marched through. Her dark curls were bursting out from beneath a dusty baseball cap and hanging down over her brown eyes. Her jeans were wore out at the knees, and her hands and cheeks were smudged with dirt.

"What's ta eat?" she bellowed.

"Nothing while you look like that," Ma said. "Go on upstairs and get cleaned up."

"But I ain't ready to come in yet," Molly protested. "I just wanted a snack."

Ma shook her head. "It's too close to supper time." Then she paused when she saw Molly eyeing the table. "But you can have a cucumber if you want."

Molly came over to the table and craned her neck to survey the offer. She stood for a long while, scowling at the cucumbers then said, "Okay."

"Go wash your hands and you can have one."

Molly slid a stepstool over to the sink and climbed up to wash her hands. Then she plucked a freshly peeled and salted cucumber from my mother's hand, cast an irritated look in my direction, and marched back out the door.

Ma just shook her head and grinned. “Actually, I think your sister would really love to see a reptile exhibit.”

“She belongs in one.”

From outside, I heard my father’s truck rumble up the driveway and come to a squeaking halt. The door opened with a rusty moan and Pa’s voice called to Molly, “Whutchya say there, Bubba?”

Molly’s voice called back (slightly full cucumber), “Hey Pa!”

“Whutchya eatin’?”

“Gumumber.”

“Oh… I see.”

Pa entered the kitchen looking more weary than usual. He was always strong and lean, but I remember his thin frame looked slightly hunched, as if he’d been carrying a great weight around all day. His brown eyes were clear and kind, and his black hair was just turning gray at the temples.

Now it was as obvious that Molly had inherited my father’s looks as I had my mother’s. People often commented on how much of a resemblance there was between Pa and Molly, and between me and Ma. However, when it came to personalities, we were quite reversed. Molly was a tomboy just like Ma, while my father and I tended to be a bit more shy.

“Hello, Ann.” He kissed Ma on the lips, then gave me a quick wink and ruffled my hair. “Hey, Jake.”

I handed him the advertisement. “Can we go see the alligators tomorrow? They’re gonna have real live ones.”

Pa read the flier and shook his head. "Well whuddaya know, honest-to-goodness live alligators. This town's gettin' to be a regular hub of exotic entertainment."

"So can we go?"

He squeezed my shoulder. "Sure, why not. I think Molly might like it too."

I remember being in such a good mood that afternoon, I started my chores without even being asked. I fed the horse and goats, cleaned the stalls, and still had time to terrorize the chickens before Ma called me in for supper. But just as she did, I heard another voice calling to me as well. Buck Miller was peddling up the driveway on his bike.

Right on schedule.

4

Now, Buck Miller, as my mother often lamented, seemed to have a 'perpetual attraction to trouble', but since there weren't many other boys my age in Silas, we had become best friends. He lived a half-mile up the road in a small, one-story house. His father drove a truck for a living and was rarely home, while his mother waitressed at a bar over in Comstock. She worked nights and usually slept most of the day. It'd been said that she could outdrink any man in the county, so looking back, I could see why my folks let Buck spend so much time at our home.

His long, brown hair was usually uncombed and he had developed a sort of twitch from constantly flinging it out of his eyes. Once every couple of months, Ma would arm-wrestle him for the privilege of 'shearing his locks' as she called it. She would also put him to work around the house every so often, helping me with the chores in exchange for the meals, that he generally ate by us as well. During school, she would pack an extra sandwich in my bag, telling me to give it to Buck if he'd forgotten his own. Pa would occasionally have us both help him with a particularly big job, like fixing the fence or digging out a stump. Then he would send Buck home with a new shirt or pair of pants as payment. While Buck tended to complain about the work, he always seemed proud of his clothes and was quick to point out the fact that he had *earned* them.

"Practical charity ain't just giving somebody a handout," Pa would tell me. "It's giving 'em a chance to earn something for themselves."

"Hi, Jake!" Buck called, as I was coming out of the barn. Then he saw my mother standing in the doorway. "Hello, Mrs. Kelly. I was wondering if Jake could go on a bike ride with me?"

"He can't right now, Buck," Ma said, as Molly squeezed past her into the house. "We're just about to sit down to supper." Then she smiled. "Would you care to join us?"

Buck hopped off his bike. "Well, I guess so. If it's not too much trouble."

"No trouble at all."

It had become a sort of ritual between my mother and Buck. He would stop by just before supper and ask if my mother if I could come outside. Ma would explain that we were getting ready to eat, and then invite him to join us. He would always accept her invitation, though he tried to look like he wasn't *expecting* the offer.

That evening we sat down to roast beef, mashed potatoes and gravy, corn on the cob, and cucumber salad. Pa said grace and we plunged into our meal. Buck ate like a horse, devouring several slices of beef and two helpings of potatoes. My parents watched with expressions that looked somewhere between pity and amusement. We were almost through with supper when I remembered what had happened earlier that afternoon.

"I saw old Abe Garner today!" I blurted out.

Buck nearly choked, while Molly continued shoveling food into her mouth, ignoring the rest of us.

"Where'd you see him?" Buck asked.

"He was heading into the grocery store," I said. "Mrs. Buckman nearly ran into him when she was coming out!"

"What'd he do?"

"Well," I said, thinking back. "He just kinda…"

"Yeah?"

"…held the door open for her."

Ma chuckled. "Well now, he does sound like a vicious sort of character. Holding a door open for a woman? Why he oughta be locked up for that."

"Aw, he's too smart to do anything in broad daylight," Buck said. He set down his fork and looked around the table like he was telling one of his ghost stories. "I heard that one time, three kids went fishin' near his place in the swamp and never came back. They didn't find their bodies for three weeks—"

"That's quite enough," Ma scowled. Then I noticed that Molly had stopped eating and was staring at Buck.

I turned to my father. "Why do you suppose he lives all alone out in the swamp?"

Pa was silent for a moment, poking at his food. Then he shrugged. "Well, I suppose a man's got a right to live anywhere he feels like. Long as he ain't hurting anyone, I guess it ain't our business where he chooses to live."

"Because Clem Anderson said he knew the *real* reason old Abe was livin' out there."

"Clem Anderson?" Ma set down her fork and sighed. "Sometimes I wish that man would just…" she stopped and bit her lower lip, "just… keep his opinions to himself."

Pa looked at me for a moment, and his eyes had the same sad look I had seen in Yancey Buckman's earlier. He shook his head. "I'm sure there's a lot of folks in Silas that don't think too highly of Mr. Garner. But most of them don't even know the man and they don't have anything better to do than to make up stories about him."

We finished the meal in silence. I wanted to ask Pa more about it, but I knew better than to keep talking about something after Ma gets the look on her face that she had gotten just then. Afterward, Pa pushed his chair back and patted his stomach.

"Well, Ann Marie Kelly, you have outdone yourself once again. I do believe that was one of the finest meals you've ever made."

"Thank you, Jack."

Then Pa gave the rest of us a stern look and we took our cue immediately.

"Delicious, Ma."

"Yup."

"That was an excellent meal, Mrs. Kelly."

As Ma began to clear the table, Buck and I headed outside. We ran down the narrow trail behind our house that cut through the field and led back toward the river. Buck and I had found a special spot at the edge of our property where we would fish and hunt for frogs. We sat on the grassy bank that overlooked the river and stared out at the slow moving water. We lay back and watched the sun turn slowly from amber to crimson as it neared the horizon. I guess we were both too full and tired to talk much, so we just chewed on grass, skipped stones into the water, and soaked in the melancholy peacefulness of the river.

After a while Buck sat up and spat out a bit of grass he'd been chewing on. "Y'ever sometimes wish you'd just wake up one morning and have a totally new family?"

"Nope," I said. "Do you?"

"Well…" Buck scratched his ear like he was searching for words. "I guess I do most mornings. I mean, I come over to your house and everything seems the way it *should* be, y'know?" He looked back at me with a curious expression. "I mean, your Pa… he comes home every night and your Ma cooks you meals and everything." He shrugged. "It just seems that's the way it's *supposed* to be."

I sat up, feeling like I should say something. "Well, I guess I never really thought about it too much before."

"That's because it's normal," Buck said. "It *should* be that way, so that's why you never notice it. Seems like you never notice how good something is 'til it gets messed up."

I opened my mouth but I couldn't find the proper thing to say. "I'm sorry," was all that came out. In an hour or so, I'd have a million right things to say, but by then it'd be too late.

Buck just shook his head and lay back. The moment had passed.

“Hey.” I perked up as an idea came to me. “Why don’t you come along with us to the Festival tomorrow? That’d be fun!”

“Mmm,” Buck sighed, his eyes closed. “We’ll see.”

Looking back, I wonder how I could’ve been so blind to Buck’s feelings. Although I knew he wasn’t happy at home, he so rarely talked about it that sometimes I’d forget how miserable he really was. Every once in a long while though, whenever he was softened by the great melancholy of the river, and when he was sure no one else was around, Buck Miller would lower his guard ever-so-slightly… and only for a moment.

But I was too self-absorbed to notice.

The sun had vanished beyond the horizon and the gray shadow of dusk was creeping over us when my mother’s voice echoed faintly, calling me back home.

5

I woke up the next morning to the sound of my mother snapping up the window shades in my room. Sunlight poured in like water bursting through a dam, washing the last shreds of sleep away. I moaned and clutched a pillow over my face as Ma pounced on the bed and shook me by the shoulders.

"Get up! Get up! It's time to get uhh-up," she sang in no particular melody. My mother truly loved to sing and did so every chance she got. Pa often remarked that whatever she may have lacked in tone, God had graciously compensated for in volume.

The whole house was filled with the smell of bacon and coffee. I pulled on my jeans and t-shirt and headed downstairs where the kitchen was bathed in the morning sunlight. We sat down to scrambled eggs, crisp shards of bacon and toasted slabs of homemade bread glistening with butter. Last and best was a pan of freshly baked cornbread. Wisps of steam floated up from its golden crust and every pore oozed with syrup. Biting into a wedge of it would send a flood of warm maple flavor rolling over your tongue.

While music may not have been my mother's specialty, Saturday morning breakfasts were among her crowning achievements. They were a kind of symphony in themselves and seemed to be her way of making up to us for having to endure the hardships of her singing.

After breakfast, I went about my chores and, just as I was finishing, Buck came speeding up the driveway on his bike.

Pa was hoisting a cooler into the back of the pickup. "Mornin' Buck," he said. "Think your ma would mind if you came to the festival with us?"

"Naw," Buck puffed, out of breath. "She's still in bed."

"Did you have any breakfast?"

"Uh… yeah, I kinda—"

"Because I think we've got some cornbread and a few slices of bacon left if you want."

"Alright!"

Buck disappeared into the house and I drew up to Pa, feeling a little sheepish. "I kinda invited Buck to come along with us. I guess I forgot to ask if it was okay with you."

"That was mighty thoughtful of you, Jake." Pa squeezed my shoulder and smiled.

I shrugged and looked down at my feet. It was one of those times in a boy's life when deep down, he knows he's happy to have made his father proud of him, though he's not quite ready to admit it.

I kicked at the dirt. "Yeah, well I guess I'm a pretty nice guy."

Pa chuckled and swatted the back of my head. "A trait you must've inherited from me."

Pa had once said that if the Silas Township Summer Festival could be captured on canvas, it'd probably look like one of Molly's finger-paintings: a colorful hodge-podge of sights, sounds and smells. Folks would come down from Comstock and Chase, and even as far away as Bilford to spend the day. The scent of roasted corn, grilled chicken and barbecued ribs filled the hot humid air as vendors prepared for an early lunch-hour rush. Packs of highschool guys strutted around the game booths trying to win stuffed animals for whoever happened to be their girlfriend that week. Jolly Meyer sat on the platform above the dunk tank, taunting and heckling the folks that had lined up to try to hit the target with a softball and dunk him. An icecream vendor pushed his cart through the crowd, advertising his treats at the top of his lungs. Above all the banter, a slightly out-of-tune brass band stumbled through a set of marching tunes. And right smack in the middle of it all stood the big red Ferris wheel, turning slowly in the midmorning sun.

We followed Pa through the crowd to the far side of the wooded picnic area along the riverfront. Several families had already staked out their territories, and he led us well beyond them to a secluded spot down near the edge of the river. Ma spread out the large blanket she had brought and Pa set the lawnchairs and cooler in the shade of a nearby tree. Then he joined my mother on the blanket to keep an eye on Molly, who had already started playing along the shoreline with her trucks.

Pa stretched out and yawned. "You boys can go walk around if you want, just be back in time for lunch."

Buck and I were already halfway back to the festival. "Okay," we shouted over our shoulders, and plunged into the crowd, weaving through the jungle of bodies.

Buck seemed distracted by all the commotion, slowing down at every booth to watch. But I tugged at his arm. I had only one thing on my mind that morning. Before I could enjoy myself or look at anything else, I had to find the reptile exhibit. We stopped for a moment in the shadow of the Ferris wheel. Its big red spokes spun slowly around, and a long line was already forming.

Buck stood with one eye shut, squinting up at the topmost seats. "You know, we'd probably get a pretty good view of the whole park from up there." He looked back at me. "That would save us some time, hunting for that alligator tent."

I sighed. While it was true, we couldn't see very much from ground level, I also knew the park wasn't that big and it wouldn't take long to find the exhibit.

"Besides," Buck continued, "that line's just gonna get longer. If we wanna ride, we'd better do it now."

I sighed. "I guess there's plenty of time to find the exhibit."

"Sure," Buck grinned and slapped my back. "We got all day."

I followed him over to the end of the line, and fifteen minutes later, we were seated in one of the buckets, slowly rotating our way upward. We paused every moment or two as new passengers climbed aboard the seats below us. This gave us plenty of time to look around at the park below. The crowd looked bigger than I had figured. People milled every which-way among the booths like a horde of rats. Our bucket slowly rolled its way to the top and soon we could even see my folks and Molly far across the park near the edge of the river.

I spotted a small circus tent in a grassy spot near the boat launch on the other side of the park. A large, white truck was backed up at one end of the tent. I could see two men unloading something, though I couldn't make out exactly what it was.

As soon as the ride was over, we made a beeline for that tent. The whole area had been fenced off, keeping folks a good twenty or thirty feet away from the tent itself. Underneath the white canopy, several rows of chairs were set up in a semicircle around a wooden stage.

The two men I had seen earlier were still busy unloading crates off the truck. One man was big and sweaty, with a crew-cut and faded blue-jeans and a white t-shirt that didn't quite cover his round belly. The other was a gangly, long-haired fellow who looked like he wouldn't have been able to lift even the smallest crate by himself.

Buck and I leaned on the fence and watched quietly for several minutes. A number of folks strolled by, pausing to see if there was anything happening.

We couldn't see any alligators or reptiles from our vantage point, and soon Buck grew restless. I was getting pretty frustrated as well, and then I heard an odd voice behind us.

"Wull there, ahn't you two a little ehly," it said. "The show doesn't staht til this afternoon."

6

We turned around and saw a tall, broad-shouldered man, dressed in a tan shirt and baggy shorts, like someone on a safari might wear. He had a square jaw and dark hair with light blue eyes that seemed even brighter against his tanned face. He glanced down at his watch and said, "You got a couple ahhs yet.

Buck and I just stared at him.

The big man leaned closer and curled up one eyebrow. "Two-thirty," he said slowly. "The show stahts at two-thirty."

Buck found his voice first. "Who are you?"

The big man straightened up and grinned. "Name's Ellis Woods, mate."

Buck's eyes narrowed and he looked at the man sideways. "Where're you from anyways?"

The man laughed. "Australia originally. But I've been living in Bilford for the last couple of years."

"Ohhh," Buck and I said together.

"You boys ever been to my alligator fahm up in Bilford?"

We glanced at each other and shook our heads.

He folded his arms and frowned. "Have you even *heard* of Gator World before?"

"No," I said. "Well, not before yesterday."

Ellis shook his head in disgust. "I spent 'aff my earnings last year on advertising and I can't even get the word aat to you blokes dan here in Silas."

I tried to explain. "Actually, I don't read the newspaper too much. But I'm sure there's plenty of folks here that've heard of you."

That didn't seem to help as Ellis just grunted to himself and shook his head again. I started feeling a little guilty and tried to make him feel better. "So… how many alligators do you have on your farm?"

He looked up. "Hmm? Oh, I got abat two hundred, not to mention all the other reptalls. All together there's abat three hundred animals. Of course, I've annly been in business for two years."

Buck's frown grew deeper. "Does everyone in Austria sound like you?"

Ellis leaned over. "It's *Australia*, mate. You know, *the land dan undah.* And y'know, to me *you're* the ones who sand funny when you talk." With that he chuckled and straightened up. "So whaddaya say? You boys wanna help set up a few pens or something? Maybe get a sneak preview?"

Well, he didn't need to ask *that* twice! We followed him through the gate to the area behind the stage. The two men who'd been unloading the truck were sitting on one of the wooden crates, each one gulping a can of beer. The crates had several holes drilled through the sides with the words DANGER: LIVE ANIMALS stenciled across the tops. The men stood up as Ellis approached.

“Fellas, I managed to recruit some help,” Ellis said and looked down at us. “Uh, y’know I don’t even know your names.”

“I’m Jake,” I said. “And this is my friend Buck.”

Ellis nodded. “Wull, Jake and Buck, these here are two of my men from GatorWorld: Max Finney and Morris Boggs.” He pointed to the skinny man and then the big one. “Boys, this here’s Buck and Jake. They were loitering around so I thought I’d put ’em to work.” He shot us a wink.

He took us to the tent where three long tables had been set up on each side of the stage. Each table had several small cages on top and each cage had a different kind of lizard or snake inside. Next, he led us out to a row of chainlink pens that had been set up behind the tent.

“We need to stake the bottom of these fences into the ground to make them more secure before we put the animals inside,” Ellis explained. “Wouldn’t do to have a gator crawl underneath and bite someone’s toes off, eh?”

He handed us a hammer and a bag of metal tent stakes, and we went about the chore gladly. Within twenty minutes or so we had finished and Finney checked our work by kicking at the bottom of the fences to make sure they were secure. Then Boggs went from cage to cage with a hose and watered down the grass inside. Finally the three of them prepared to transfer the animals from their crates into the pens.

“You boys stand back a bit,” Ellis cautioned as they slid the first crate over to the nearest pen. The crate was the size of a small coffin. Ellis unlatched the lid and slowly opened it up.

Buck and I craned our necks, but we couldn't see anything at first. Then Ellis reached inside and produced a small alligator. It was about three feet long from its snout to the tip of its tail. It had a black, leathery hide with a pale underbelly and its jaws had been tied shut with some sort of muzzle. It squirmed and jerked about in his grasp but he had its body secure under one arm. With his free hand he held the jaws shut while Finney undid the muzzle and then he carefully plopped it down inside the pen.

Buck and I looked at each other skeptically. This didn't seem too dangerous of a creature, certainly nothing to be afraid of. We watched as they transferred a second alligator, about the same size, into the pen. The two little gators stood nose to nose with each other, not moving a bit as Ellis took a third one from the crate, and then a fourth.

They moved on to the second pen where they pulled a slightly larger alligator from its crate. This one looked to be about four or five feet in length and it took both Ellis and Boggs to hold it still while Finney undid the muzzle.

We watched them fill each pen with alligators of different sizes. Some would lay very still wherever they had been plopped. Others scurried around the pens, nipping at their cell mates. Eventually, they slowed down as well and just lay there with the rest, basking in the sunlight.

The last crate was the largest of all, and took the three of them to slide it inside the remaining cage through a narrow gate in one corner. This particular crate opened from the end instead of the top like the others.

Ellis carefully reached in and grabbed the end of a rope. He tugged and pulled and after a few moments a large muzzled snout appeared. Next, came two eyes and a thick, leathery neck. Ellis continued to pull and yank until finally the entire beast emerged into the sunlight.

"Whoa," Buck and I gasped.

7

Ellis grinned, wiped his brow, and gestured down at the animal. "This here's Brutus. He's a nine-footer I caught down in the Everglades last year."

The big gator just lay there, its sides moving slowly in and out as it breathed.

"We keep him well fed so he stays nice and lethargic. We don't want him getting too hungry while he's out in public."

He reached down and unbuckled the muzzle but the big gator still didn't move.

They closed up the gate, and then set about adding wooden barriers around each pen so no one could lean on the fences or reach down inside. Finally, they put up warning signs at each cage to tell folks not to get too close.

Just about that time I looked at my watch and gasped. It was five minutes after noon and we were late for lunch. As much as I hated to leave, I knew it wouldn't be wise to upset my folks, so Buck and I excused ourselves and headed back.

Pa was stretched out on the blanket when we returned with his head resting on my mother's lap. She was curling a lock of his dark brown hair with her fingers. A stack of sandwiches were set out on a paper plate with a bag of potato chips and celery sticks and sodas in the middle of the blanket. Molly played with her toy truck in the grass nearby.

"You'll never guess what we got to do!" I exclaimed as we arrived.

Pa tilted up his sunglasses. "What's that?"

"We got to help set up the pens for the alligators," Buck said. "And we even got to watch while they put 'em inside!"

"And we got to talk to Ellis Woods," I added. "He's from Australia and he showed us all the lizards and snakes—"

"And he's got an alligator *nine feet long*!"

"Maybe we can go to GatorWorld up in Bilford sometime—"

"Hold on." Pa put up his hands. "You can tell us all about it while we eat. Right now, I'm starving."

Ma called Molly over and Pa prayed. "Lord, thank you for this food you provided for us. Thank you for Ma who prepared it all. And thanks too, for the good weather and the fun we can have today. Amen."

Ma made sure we washed our hands with the little bar of soap she had and the water from the cooler we had brought.

Buck and I took turns telling all the details of our experience with Ellis Woods while we ate. We described all the alligators to them, especially Brutus, who even got Molly's attention.

Afterwards, Pa stood up, stretched, and yawned. "Well," he said, "everybody ready to go see the fair?"

We helped clean up and fold the blanket. Then we set everything in a pile beneath the tree and headed back to the festival. As we waded through the crowded park, my folks each held one of Molly's hands, and she swung between them more than she actually walked.

Buck and I tried our skill at some of the carnival games. Pa won a stuffed bear for Molly that was nearly as big as she was, and Ma managed to dunk Jolly Meyer with her first shot. Everybody applauded and she got a gift certificate for a restaurant up in Chase.

By the time two-thirty rolled around, Buck and I led the way to the reptile exhibit. There were plenty of folks already inside the tent area looking at all the cages, and we spent some time looking around. I felt kind of like a tour guide, since I had seen almost everything beforehand.

I told them all about the lizards and snakes, even though I didn't really know all that much. The exit that led to the alligator pens behind the tent had been roped off with a sign that said it would be open after the show.

After a few minutes, Ellis Woods appeared on the stage speaking through a small PA system.

"G'day, g'day everyone," he said with a big, toothy grin. He wore a widebrimmed hat with one side curled up. "If you'll all be good enough to find your seats, we'll get started straight away."

The crowd moved back toward the chairs. Several kids dashed for the front seats, and their parents started scolding them. We found some seats near the stage, just off to one side. After a few minutes, the commotion died down and Ellis continued.

"My name's Ellis Woods. I'm originally from Australia. I'm what you might call a zoologist, which means I study animals. My particular interest is in reptiles. Today, I'll be introducing you to a number of strange lookin' critters that I've encountered along my travels, and that are now on exhibit at Gator World."

At that point Ellis asked for a show of hands to see how many folks had ever been to Gator World. About a half-dozen people raised their hands, and I could see a brief scowl flash across his face.

"Wull, now that you've heard where it is, I expect you to come up and give us a visit."

He went on to talk about what it was like to grow up in Australia, and about someplace called the *outback*, and all the snakes and crocodiles that lived there. He talked about how he had gone to college to learn more about reptiles, and he even showed us some scars on his leg from where he'd been bitten by a crocodile when he was younger. Then he started to tell us about Gator World and all the different animals he had there for folks to come and see.

With that, Boggs came out carrying a large iguana about three feet long. Ellis talked for a few minutes about iguanas, and had some kids in the front row come up to pet it. Next, Finney came out with a large snake that looked to be about eight feet long. Ellis held it up for everyone to see. Its bright pink tongue flicked out at us like a tiny party favor. Ellis explained about how snakes use their tongues to smell, and what kinds of things they eat. After he had finished, he handed the snake back to Finney, and stepped out to the edge of the stage.

"Wull now," he said, rubbing his hands together. "I'm sure most of you want to see some alligators, am I right?"

Some folks started clapping, and Boggs came out carrying one of the smaller gators. He handed it to Ellis who showed it to the crowd.

"Now this little bloke is one of your common North American alligators. There's quite a few of these guys livin' in the rivers and swamps in this part of the country. Of course, most of 'em are quite a bit larger than this one here." He walked across the front of the stage showing the little alligator to the kids in the front rows. He talked about how big alligators get, and how many of them he had at Gator World. Then he took out a pen and tapped the gator's snout lightly. Its little jaws opened up wide.

"This is what zoologists technically refer to as the dangerous end of an alligator," Ellis said, as the audience laughed politely. He brought the pen just inside the gaping jaws. Suddenly, we heard a sound like a cork popping from a bottle as the gator's jaws snapped shut, clamping down hard on the pen.

Ellis pried the pen loose and looked back out at the crowd. "As you can imagine, it's a good idea to keep your fingers out of his way. Especially if you meet one of his big brothers somewhere."

With that he asked for a volunteer to help him with a demonstration and almost every hand in the audience went up. He looked across the crowd and his eyes settled in our direction. Both Buck and I were on our feet with our hands as high as we could hold them. We just knew he'd call on one of us. But he didn't seem to notice us at all.

"How about you there," Ellis said, pointing just to our right. And then I saw that my mother had her hand up as well.

She jumped up and shot us a mocking grin as she marched up to the stage.

Ellis was clutching the young alligator in one hand and holding its jaws shut with the other. When Ma got up on stage he smiled and nodded at her. "G'day."

"G'day," Ma said back.

"I'd like you to get the roll of electrical tape out of my shirt pocket and wrap a long piece around this fella's snout once or twice."

Ma hesitated for a moment, raising an eyebrow at him. Then she removed the roll of tape and started to do as he had asked. Just as she reached out with the piece of tape, Ellis jiggled the little gator. "Careful!" he said.

Ma let out a shriek and jumped back. Everyone laughed.

"Just kidding." Ellis grinned, winking at the audience.

Ma gave him an unamused look, gathered her courage again, and wrapped the tape twice around the gator's snout. Then Ellis handed Ma the gator and made her hold it herself. She looked a little uneasy but managed a nervous smile.

"While an alligator has a very powerful bite," Ellis said. "It doesn't have nearly as much strength to open its jaws and even a piece of tape can keep this one's mouth closed."

With that, Finney came out carrying one of the five-foot gators. He set it down and took the smaller alligator from Ma. Ellis thanked Ma for her cooperation and the crowd applauded politely as she sat back down.

Pa looked at her thoughtfully for a second. Then he shook his head and chuckled like he always did whenever Ma did something that surprised him, and he knew deep down it really shouldn't have.

Ellis picked up the leash of the larger gator and pulled the animal gently to the front of the stage. "Now an alligator is actually a pretty shy animal for the most part," he said. "And he'll usually leave you alone if you don't bother *him*. But they're still not an animal you'd want to get too close to out in the wild."

He went on for a few more minutes, revealing all sorts of facts about alligators and other reptiles. Then he finished up by inviting everyone to take a walk by the pens behind the tent, and especially to come up to Gator World for a visit.

After the show, we went out to take a look at the alligators. Buck and I continued being tour guides by explaining how we had helped to make the fences secure. When we got to big Brutus's pen, we found him basking in the sun. A lot of folks were gathered around his cage but the big gator didn't seem to notice them. His black, leathery sides just moved slowly in and out as he breathed. After a while most of the folks moved on, chuckling to themselves about how they weren't even sure the gator was alive at all. Finally, Pa said we should get going as well.

We walked around the carnival for a while more, looking at the booths and craft exhibits. Pa carried Molly up on his shoulders as he walked along. She had been fascinated by the smaller gators, and kept talking about how cute she thought they were.

"Can we buy one Pa?" she asked.

"No sir, Bubba," Pa said. "Didn't you hear the man? Gators don't make good pets."

"Why not?"

"Because little gators grow up to be *big* gators, and big gators *eat* little girls!" With that, he snatched Molly down from his shoulders and folded her up in his arms, squeezing and tickling her as if she was in the jaws of a big, toothless alligator.

Molly giggled and laughed for a moment, but then grew serious. "Like that little girl up in Chase?"

Pa stopped and his smile faded away like the sun when it gets hidden behind a cloud. He propped Molly up on the crook of his arm and looked at her thoughtfully for a moment.

"You heard about that, did you?"

She nodded. "Yep."

Pa chewed the inside of his cheek like he did whenever he was pondering something. His eyes had a faraway look in them, and just a little sad. After a moment he nodded and looked back at Molly. "Yeah. Just like that little girl."

8

It had been earlier that spring that we had heard the news of Tom Hatcher's seven-year-old daughter, Sarah Mae, being taken under by a big gator. The two of them had been fishing just south of Chase where Hickman Creek joins up with the Shawno River. The paper said Tom had gone up to his car for a moment when he heard a great splashing sound, and then his daughter screamed. When he got back, Sarah Mae had disappeared, and all he remembered seeing was the back of a huge alligator swimming off downstream. They dragged the river all the way down to Comstock, but never found any sign of his daughter's body. A couple days later, they shot a big ten-foot gator which they said was the one that had killed Sarah Mae. A week later, Tom had his house up for sale. They say he moved up north somewhere.

Needless to say, since then folks had been very cautious about letting their kids go too near the river. Sheriff Mason had spent the better part of six weeks trying to assure folks that this had just been an isolated incident and not something to cause a panic.

We had all grown pretty quiet, and then Ma reached up and tugged at Molly's curls. "But don't worry none," she said. "We're not gonna let any gator get *you* okay?"

"Okay," Molly said.

We walked about the fair a bit more, and then headed back to the picnic sight to grill some hamburgers for supper. Pa had brought charcoal, and made a fire in a fire pit nearby. And Ma had made some potato salad and brownies. The five of us ate supper and watched the sun reflecting off the river just down below us. A warm breeze swept up from the south and carried with it all the familiar smells of summertime. I lay back and watched the branches above us sway back and forth in the breeze. My folks talked about some of the projects they wanted to get done around the house over the summer while Buck and Molly played with Molly's trucks under a juniper tree down near the river.

I was nearly drifting off to sleep when Pa jostled me with his foot.

"Whutchya say Jake," he said, "you wanna toss the softball around a bit?"

I sat up and rubbed my eyes. "Sure."

Pa dropped my glove down on my lap. He stood over me pounding a softball into his own glove. He motioned to an open area along the river. "Go out yonder."

I ran out a ways and we played catch for a while.

"You been practicing for your league this summer?" Pa asked.

"Yeah, but I need to work on my fielding more. I'd like to play third base this year."

Pa nodded. "Billy Meyer ain't likely to give up his position without a fuss. You best show you can field grounders better'n he can."

I shrugged. "Billy's gettin' kinda chunky since he's been going with Frannie Becker. I don't think he can bend over so well no more."

Pa chuckled. "Yeah, a good woman'll do that to ya. You just watch so you don't find yourself a sweetheart who makes you take her out for donuts and icecream and such."

I laughed and we threw for a while more.

"Let me give you some with a little pepper to 'em," Pa said after a bit.

My Pa had quite an arm for a man nearing forty. He used to play left field in the men's county league and he once threw a man out at home plate from deep in left-center when he was in high school. Folks still talk about his arm to this day.

He wound up and let one go. I caught it smack in the center of my glove and winced.

Pa raised an eyebrow. "Did that hurt?"

"Naw," I said, swallowing hard and tossing the ball back. "Ma throw's harder'n that."

Pa tossed the ball up to himself and chuckled. "Sure, but that one was only as hard as I throw to Molly in the backyard. *This* one'll be like one I'd throw to your ma."

He reeled back and let it sail. For an instant, all I could see was a white blur coming straight towards me. I could tell right away that it was going to sail over my head. I jumped up to catch it but the ball streaked by an inch above my glove and disappeared into the trees behind me.

We stood silently for a few seconds, watching the trees, almost as if we expected the ball to come flying back out at us all by itself. I looked back at Pa who was chewing on the inside of his cheek again.

"You're s'posed to catch those," he said.

I cocked an eyebrow and grunted.

We made our way into the tall weeds beyond the trees, trying to estimate where the ball might have landed. The ground dropped off down a steep bank where it met the river. Below us, a thick patch of cattails sprung up in the muddy shallows of the water.

"You don't suppose it landed in the water?" I asked.

"Well, I don't see it…" Pa craned his neck and peered down. "Yep, there it is." He pointed to a pale, round object nestled in the weeds, a few yards off shore.

Pa took off his shoes, rolled up his trousers, and made his way down the muddy embankment into the water. He winced as he stepped on some rocks along the bottom, and waded out to where the ball was floating.

Just as he got within reach, he sank down to his waist into the water. I stood on the bank, laughing. The drop-off had taken him by surprise, and he lost his balance slightly. He quickly steadied himself and grabbed hold of the ball.

"I didn't realize it was so deep here," he said, turning around to toss the ball back to me.

But I saw the weeds begin to sway in an odd motion, as if a strong wind was blowing through them. It looked like the whole patch of mud and cat-tails was slowly coming to life.

Suddenly, a huge, black shape burst up from out of the water. It moved so quickly, at first it didn't even seem real. For an instant, I couldn't tell what it was. But then its black jaws opened to reveal a large pink tongue and a jagged row of yellow teeth, and with a sudden horror I knew…

An alligator!

But it looked as big as a truck! It rose up from the water, and my eyes darted along its thick black hide trying to find where it ended. I couldn't even see its tail. It seemed to go on forever like some monster out of a nightmare! My body felt like it had turned to ice. All I could do was watch as the animal plowed into my father, knocking him off balance. Its massive jaws clamped down across his waist. Then it twisted its great bulk around and pulled him backward off his feet.

Pa looked like a child in its jaws, and not a grown man at all. I could see him grasping at the creature's snout, but in a matter of seconds, it had dragged him out into deeper water.

My head was a fog of fear and confusion. I kept thinking to myself, it'll let him go. It'll let go, and Pa will be fine. He'll swim back to shore and he'll be fine…

But that didn't happen.

The last thing I saw of my father was his bare feet, limp, as they disappeared beneath the surface.

My lips moved to form the word but my voice didn't come at first. "Pa?"

The water churned furiously, and I could see only brief glimpses of a huge shadow, twisting and writhing beneath the surface out in the middle of the river. At last a thick, ridged tail curled up out of the water and slapped back down again.

I could hear my own voice crying out, "*Pa!*"

But it sounded so odd to my ears—like someone else calling to me, far off in the distance. A shrill, high-pitched shriek that I barely recognized.

And then, as quickly as it had begun, the water grew calm and my father was gone

9

I ran back to where Ma was watching Molly and Buck. My legs felt heavy and awkward, like when you're having a nightmare and you're trying to run away from something, but you can't seem to move fast enough. It was as if everything I had just seen was all part of a bad dream, and I was praying to wake up. The corners of my vision had darkened and blurred, and my heart pounded so hard, I felt like it was going to burst out of my ribs.

"God," I kept praying. "Don't let him die. *Please* don't let him die!"

Ma sat on the blanket with her arms wrapped around her knees. A patch of late afternoon sunlight streamed down through the trees and looked like a halo all around her. The whole world seemed to be moving in slow motion. She turned her head to look at me as I ran up. She smiled, and at first her face was all at peace. But her smile faded into a look of curiosity. Curiosity changed to concern, and concern to fear.

"Jake, what's wrong."

The sound of her voice jolted me out of my daze. She got up and looked past me. "Where's your father?"

"Pa's…" I gasped for air, and couldn't find the right words to say. "There was an… an alligator in the river…" I knew I had to try to make sense to her or she would just get mad. "It got Pa and dragged him under."

She took me by the shoulders and jerked me upright. She looked right at me and I had never seen her look so serious.

"Where?"

I pointed back to the trees. Ma clutched me by the arm and called over to Buck. "Stay here and watch Molly. And *stay away from the river*!"

She ran with me in tow back toward the riverbank. For a moment, I thought maybe I had imagined the whole thing and Pa would come walking through the trees to meet us. But he never did.

We got to the edge of the bank, and I pointed down at the patch of reeds. "Right there. He went down to get the ball."

The softball was still there, perched in the weeds.

"Stay here," Ma said and made her way down to the edge of the water. "Jack!" she called. "*Jack*!" She turned back at me. "Are you *sure* this is where he was?"

"Ma," I pleaded, "I *saw* him. He was right there in the water and this gator came outta those weeds and dragged him under."

She looked back out across the water to see any trace of where Pa might be floating. Then she turned back to me. Her eyes were wide and her voice trembled slightly. "Jake, go and get help."

I just stood there for a second, not knowing what kind of help to get or where exactly to get it. Most of all, I didn't want to leave in case Pa suddenly came back and needed me. But Ma turned back to me a moment later.

"Go *now*!"

I took off, running as fast as I could.

"What happened?" Buck asked as I sprinted past him and Molly.

I didn't answer him. I didn't know what to say, and I didn't have time to stop and figure out how to say it. He stared at me with a curious expression on his face. I could tell that he wanted to come with me, but Molly was holding his hand, and I think he knew better than to leave her.

I ran through the picnic area without really knowing where I was going. Most everyone in town was down at the festival, so that was the direction I figured I should head. The picture of my father in the jaws of that alligator flashed into my mind again, and I started praying once more.

"Please God, don't let him be dead… *please*."

My foot caught on a tree root and I felt myself sprawling forward. Just before I hit the ground, an arm reached out and grabbed me around my waist.

"Whoa there pal," a voice said. "Better slow down or you're gonna break your neck."

I looked up and saw Frank Bussie grinning down at me with his long sideburns and black hair that he liked to grease back. He worked up at the mill with Pa, but he also volunteered for the fire squad in Silas. I had nearly landed on him and Lenora Delwicky while they were having their own picnic not too far from where ours had been. He hoisted me back upright.

"Hey there, Jake," he chuckled. "You nearly took a dive into Lenora's potato salad. Where're you off to in such a hurry?"

"I gotta get help!" I blurted out. "My Pa got attacked by an alligator!"

Frank's grin faded and he grabbed me by the shoulders just like Ma had done.

"What? Where is he?"

I pointed back to the trees. "It dragged him under, he—he's gone!"

Frank turned to Lenora. "Go get the Sheriff. Last I saw, he was judging pies over at the softball diamond. Jake, you show me where your Pa was."

I ran back to the riverbank for the second time, explaining to Frank as we went along. "He went in to get the softball and this big gator grabbed hold of him and dragged him under."

We got up to the edge of the bank where Ma was still searching. She looked up at us and her voice trembled even more now.

"Frank," she said. "I don't know… this is where Jake said he was… but I don't see any sign of him anywhere."

Frank looked up and down the riverbank. He motioned for me to stay put while he climbed down to the water's edge. "I had Lenora get the Sheriff. He should be here any minute." He looked back up at me. "Where exactly did you see him go under?"

"Right straight out there," I said, pointing to where the softball was floating. "The gator came outta them weeds there and bit him right across the waist. Then it pulled him backwards, down under the water."

Frank looked out at the water and then back at me. He looked as though he didn't hardly believe me at all. "How big *was* this thing?"

I shook my head. "I don't know exatcly. It was *huge*. Pa looked like a little kid compared to it."

Frank stared at me for a second longer, then at Ma, then back out at the river.

He sent Ma up in one direction and he went a little ways in the other. They called out for Pa and peered into the water. Frank wouldn't let Ma go into the river because he said there might be other gators still lurking around.

By this time, four more people had come over. They were two older couples who must've been from out of town, because I didn't recognize them at all.

"Do you need any help?" said one of the men, a tall man with glasses.

Frank glanced up at them. "Well, yes," he began. "We think a man may have been attacked by an alligator."

The two women gasped. "Oh my," said one, holding her hands to her mouth.

"That's terrible!" exclaimed the other.

Just then, Buck walked up with Molly. "Jake," he whispered. "What happened?"

"My Pa…" I began, but then I saw Molly looking up at me. She seemed confused by all the commotion, and I wasn't sure how to explain things quite yet.

"Where's Pa?" she asked.

Before I could answer her, we heard a rumbling behind us. We turned to see the flashing lights of the Sheriff's truck as it slowly made its way through the picnic area, weaving between the trees and tables. A crowd of people followed behind it.

Rooster Mason had been sheriff in Chase County for as long as I could remember. He got out of his truck and walked up to the riverbank. He stood with his hands on his hips, surveying the scene while he picked a bit of food out of his teeth with his tongue. He was a stocky, solid man with a firm jaw and gray hair, and he always looked like he was headed somewhere important.

Rooster's deputy, Billy Ray Martin, and Lenora Delwicky got out the other door. The crowd of folks that had been following them now started to draw up around us. Frank climbed back up the bank and helped Ma up as well. When Ma saw the crowd of people, and that Buck had brought Molly along, she looked cross at first. Then her face softened a little and she picked Molly up in her arms.

"Where's Pa?" Molly asked again.

Ma just shook her head and hugged Molly close. "I don't know, honey."

Rooster scratched the back of his neck. "Whuch ya say, Frank?"

"Well," Frank said, keeping his voice low, "it sounds like Jack Kelly's been attacked by an alligator. His shoes were on the bank but other than that, I haven't seen any sign of him."

The whole crowd gasped and started murmuring but Rooster ignored them.

"Did you see what happened?" he asked Frank.

"No, just his boy, Jake saw it."

Rooster put his meaty hand on my shoulder and squatted down to look me in the eye. "Son, you mind tellin' me exactly what you saw?"

I sighed and explained the story for the third time, trying to remember every detail. I could hear my voice shaking, and I started feeling like I was outside myself somehow, listening to someone else talk. My thoughts bumped around like a pinball.

When I finished, Rooster straightened up, rubbed his jaw and looked out across the water for a moment. Then he turned around again and his face was all business-like.

"Alright, Frank, I want you to get a few men together and search down the shoreline. Take one of the radios along and let me know if you find anything. More'n likely, Jack swam ashore downstream a ways, probably he's just a little scraped up and bruised is all."

Frank nodded and motioned to a couple of men in the crowd who were also on the volunteer fire squad.

Rooster turned to his deputy. "Billy Ray, your brother still got his boat in the water?"

Billy Ray nodded. "Sure does."

"Alright, I want you to round up everyone here that's got a boat and organize an *orderly* search of the river—we don't need no more accidents today. Have 'em spread out and search from this point on down to the bridge. And we're gonna need every high-powered flashlight you can get your hands on."

Billy Ray nodded and turned to the crowd. "Alright folks, I need anyone who's got a boat here to follow me…"

His voice trailed off, and Rooster turned to another man in the crowd. "Ben, I want you to get Fred Stafford and tell him to open up the hardware store. Tell him we're gonna need to borrow those portable spotlights he's been advertising. Get one to each boat."

The man nodded and ran off. Rooster called after him. "And every battery he's got. And if he gives you any guff, you tell him it's an emergency. Tell him I sent you."

Rooster rubbed his jaw again, as though there was something he'd forgotten to do. He turned around and saw Ma standing there, holding Molly.

"Don't worry, Ann," he said, still in his firm tone. "Jack's a strong swimmer—he'll be alright. If I know him, he's probably swam into town already and gettin' himself a pair of alligator boots made up as we speak."

Ma took a deep breath and nodded. "I appreciate all you're doing Sheriff."

They searched for Pa on into the evening. The sky turned from blue to purple and then to black but still no one had found anything. Rooster stayed in touch with Frank and Billy Ray over the radios but they just kept saying that they hadn't seen any sign of Pa yet.

Yancey and Clara Buckman brought over lawnchairs and blankets for us to sit on. Someone else had brought coffee. A lot of folks came by to say some words of encouragement and that they were praying for us, but as the evening grew later, I could tell Ma was having a difficult time trying not to look worried. Most of the crowd had gone home when it got dark. Only a handful of people stayed, mostly folks from church. They set up some lanterns, and talked and prayed quietly together while we waited to hear any news.

The boats had spread out across the river and we could see their lights sweeping back and forth over the water. They searched all the way down to the bridge and back, and then Rooster sent them out again. This time he told them to go on past the bridge as far as they could.

It was after ten o'clock when Frank Bussie and his group returned looking tired and discouraged. "We searched the shoreline all the way down to the bridge," he told the sheriff. "But we didn't see any sign of him."

Finally, Rooster came over to us. He looked down and kicked at the dirt a bit. "Ann, why don't you let Frank here take you and the kids home—"

Ma shook her head. "I can't leave, Rooster. You know I can't—"

Rooster raised his hands. "Now Ann, I know how bad you want to stay, but you got to think of your kids. There's not much you can do here and it's getting late."

Ma glanced down at Molly, sleeping in her arms, then back to Rooster. "Please don't ask me to leave," she whispered.

Rooster shook his head. "Now we're gonna search all night if we have to. I'll let you know the minute I hear anything, okay?"

"C'mon Ann," Frank said, "let me drive you home. Lenora can follow us in your truck."

Ma was quiet for a long while. She just stared into the light of one of the lanterns. I guess she realized that there really was nothing more she could do. I didn't want to leave either. To me it felt as if we were just giving up but I didn't say a word. I didn't talk to anyone the whole evening, not even to Buck. I just sat on the ground wrapped in a blanket holding Pa's shoes.

At length, Ma sighed and nodded. We gathered our things and carried them back to the truck. Then we piled into Frank's car and drove away. I watched the lanterns glowing faintly up at the riverbank before they disappeared from view. Ma sat in the front seat next to Frank, and in the darkness, I tried to imagine that it was her and Pa sitting together and that we were a normal family again.

10

No one spoke the whole way home. The house was completely dark because we had expected to get home before nightfall and didn't leave any lights on.

That's what we had expected.

Lenora pulled up behind us in Pa's truck. They helped us unload everything and bring it into the house. Frank said he'd drive Buck home, so they put his bike in the trunk and prepared to drive off. I could see Buck sitting alone in the back seat just staring straight ahead.

"I'll get back to the park after I drop Buck off," Frank said, as he put the car into reverse.

"Thank you for everything you did tonight, Frank," Ma said, quietly. She was holding Molly who was still asleep.

As the car backed out and drove away, we stood there in the silence. I had never heard our place so quiet before. Not even the crickets were chirping, it seemed.

Finally, Ma put her hand on my head. "Come on Jake. Get ready for bed."

I got undressed and brushed my teeth while Ma tucked Molly into bed. Everything seemed so normal, and yet so wrong. I brushed my teeth like I did every night—like I had done every night for my whole life—but tonight Pa wasn't here, and I had the feeling that he would never be here again. But still I brushed my teeth. My reflection in the mirror seemed like a stranger staring back at me, a strange boy with hollow eyes and a blank expression.

Ma came in to pray with me that night. She knelt at my bedside like she and Pa did every night. Usually, I'd pray first and then they would finish. But tonight I didn't know what to say. I felt like we should be somewhere else doing something else. But there we were just like normal.

Except Pa wasn't there.

"Dear God…" I started. My voice sounded strange like somebody else was speaking. Then my mind went blank. Usually, I had a list of things that I'd pray for, but tonight I couldn't think of any of them. I struggled for a way to put what I was feeling into words. I had always felt comfortable praying with my folks because I always knew what to say. It wasn't so much like actually talking *to* anyone as it was just talking. But now it was different. Now it was as if I had to speak to someone I had never spoken to before…

And I couldn't think of a thing to say.

"Please don't let my Pa be dead."

I looked up at Ma and I saw that her face looked just like the one I had seen in the mirror; empty and expressionless.

"Lord," she said, softly, "I know you have a reason for everything, but I have to confess, I don't know what you're trying to do right now. Please…"

Her voice cracked and she buried her head in her arms. I had never seen her like this before and I didn't know what to do. I put my hand on her arm and she took hold of it and squeezed.

"Please help us get through this," she said.

I climbed into bed. Ma ran her hand through my hair and kissed my forehead. "Good night Jake."

I lay awake and stared into the darkness. In my mind, I went over everything that had happened that afternoon. I kept thinking if only Pa hadn't gone into the river, he'd be here right now. If only that ball had landed in the grass instead of the water, he'd still be with us tonight. If only I…

If only I had caught that ball.

You're suppose to catch those.

Pa's words came back to me and hit me like a kick in the stomach. I should have caught that ball. In my mind, I saw that ball coming at me again. This time, I jumped a split-second sooner—and an inch higher—and the ball sank right into my glove. We never even went near the river. Pa was in the other room right now with Ma.

It would've been that simple. As simple as jumping a moment sooner or a few inches higher. If I had at least been able to deflect the ball a little, it might have landed in the grass, and not in the water. But I didn't react in time.

You're supposed to catch those.

In the dark, my memory played back like a movie, over and over. A hundred times, I saw that ball flying at me. A hundred times, I jumped up and the ball sailed past me and into the river. A hundred times, the alligator exploded up out of the reeds and barreled into Pa like a truck. A hundred times, I saw the look on his face…

I glimpsed his face just before he got pulled under. It wasn't pain or fear or anger. He just looked surprised and slightly curious, as though he wasn't sure what was happening to him.

My thoughts were interrupted by the sound of a truck pulling up the driveway. I glanced at my clock. It was nearly two in the morning. I threw off my blanket and tiptoed down the hallway to the stairs. Sitting on the steps, I peered down through the railing into the kitchen. The small fluorescent light over the sink was on and Ma was sitting at the table facing the door. A second later, there was a soft knock and Rooster Mason stepped inside.

He tugged off his hat and held it by the brim in front of him. He just stood there for a long while not saying a word. Ma stared at him and shook her head.

"Please don't say he's dead," I heard her pleading softly. "Please don't say that."

Rooster looked down at his feet. "I'm awful sorry, Ann." He shifted his weight. "They found him—his… his body… just after one o'clock."

His words crashed into me like a tidal wave.

Ma put her face in her hands and started to sob. Rooster came over and placed one of his big arms around her shoulders, and in that moment she looked like a little girl, sobbing uncontrollably. She wept for a long while and Rooster stood there the whole time, trying to comfort her.

That night, something inside of me broke. As I watched my mother crying at the kitchen table, I felt like I was watching a movie. It was as if I was outside myself again, looking in at someone else's hurt. But I didn't feel a thing. I knew I should be crying too but no tears came.

Ma looked up and asked through her sobs, "Was it… was it an alligator?"

Rooster nodded. "It looks that way. We're gonna wait and see what Doc Graham says."

"First that little girl up in Chase, and now Jack," Ma said, almost angrily. "We haven't had a single death from a gator in over ten years in this county. Now we've had two in less than three months. What's happening Rooster?"

Rooster shook his head. "I don't know, Ann. I talked with that fella who owns the alligator farm up in Bilford. He's offered to help with the search while he's in town. He's the one who found the gator that killed the Hatcher girl so I'm hoping he can tell us more."

Ma wiped her eyes and squared her shoulders. "I want to see his body, I… I have to see him."

Rooster straightened up and shook his head. "Ann, he… he's tore up pretty bad—"

"I *have* to."

"Don't do that to yourself, Ann," he said. "Remember him the way you last saw him. That's how you should remember him, not… not like this."

Ma sobbed again for several more minutes.

"What am I going to do?" she said after a while. "How am I going to tell the kids?"

"You ain't alone in this, Ann," Rooster said. "There ain't a body in town that don't know and love you two. Jack was a good man. He's helped out plenty of folks over the years, and now it's their turn to help you. If you need anything at all, you just call. Milly and me'd be more than willing to help out."

"Thank you, Rooster." Ma stood up and wiped her eyes again. "I appreciate all you've done tonight."

She gave him a hug and walked him to the door.

"You sure you don't need anything tonight?" Rooster asked as he put his hat back on.

Ma shook her head. "I called my sister in Atlanta when I got home. She and her husband are driving down tonight. They'll be here in the morning."

Rooster nodded. "Right." Then he hugged Ma again and said, "Remember, you ain't alone, Ann."

With that, he stepped out into the night. Ma closed the door and leaned her back against it. She stood there, motionless, for a long time. Then I could see her tears start to flow again. She sank down to the floor and sat, hugging her knees, and weeping softly.

11

I stepped out quietly into the chilly morning air. The moon hung fat and full over the trees. Ma had gone to bed over an hour ago but I couldn't sleep at all. I snuck out to the barn and pulled out my bike. I had to go back.

Something was calling me back.

It wasn't a voice speaking out loud, but it called me clear enough. I headed back into town. The streets were empty and dark, and the buildings looked like they'd been deserted for years. I passed through Silas, down the highway for a quarter of a mile, and turned on the gravel road that led back to the park. I wove between the booths that were all locked up for the night, past the ferris wheel, and into the picnic area.

A light wind blew through the trees. The leaves rustled and the branches clacked in the night.

The voice inside me was growing stronger.

I stopped back at the riverbank and looked out over the rippling water.

"*Jake.*"

The voice was so soft, I wasn't even sure I had actually heard it at first.

"*Jake*."

I looked down.

Pa was lying there in the reeds!

Horror ran through my veins like ice water. "*Pa*!" I tried to shout, but all I could manage was a hoarse whisper. I scrambled down the bank and splashed into the cold water. Relief flooded over me. "They said you were dead!"

Pa looked up at me, his face was pale and bleeding. "Help me…"

"They said they found your body—"

"Please…" Pa rasped.

I threw my arms around him and hugged him. "I love you Pa. I love—"

I stopped. Something wasn't right. There was something else in the water—I couldn't see anything, but I could *feel* it.

Then, in the moonlight I saw it. A giant black shadow stirred in the reeds just a few yards away! It was like the whole river was coming to life and crawling toward us. Yellow snake-eyes glowed in the darkness. Huge jaws opened.

I wrapped my arms around Pa's chest and pulled, but he felt heavy and limp.

"Come on," I screamed. "Move your legs!"

Pa stared blankly up at me. "Help… me."

I tugged at his arms, trying to slide him onto shore. I lost my grip and slipped backward into the mud. The gator's jaws clamped down on Pa's leg and started to drag him back into the water.

"Help me, Jake!" Pa rasped, clawing at the mud.

I lunged forward and grabbed his hand.

"*Please… help me… Jake…*"

I clung to him with all my strength, and dug my feet into the mud.

"I can't hold on, Pa!" I sobbed. I had just found him and now I was losing him all over again.

"Jake," he said in a hoarse whisper. "*Jake…*"

Then his hand slipped from mine, and he disappeared into the water…

I sat up in bed, gasping for air. It was still dark outside. A cold sweat soaked my shirt and my heart pounded inside my chest. The sheets were twisted around my legs as I clutched a pillow to my chest.

The vision of my nightmare faded, and the memories of the previous day seeped back into my mind. The festival… the river… the alligator…

I sat in the dark for a long while, until my heart stopped pounding. I looked at my clock. It was three-thirty and Pa was dead.

The house stood dark and silent. A light breeze blew through my open window. I shivered and pulled the covers over my head. I lay there for a long while, afraid to go back to sleep, afraid to dream again. But I felt exhausted and eventually, I drifted off once more to sleep.

When I woke up again, the sun was shining and I could hear the clanging of pots and dishes down in the kitchen.

Ma was cooking breakfast, just like normal.

I got dressed and went downstairs. Molly sat on the sofa in the living room with her truck at her feet. But this morning she didn't look very interested in playing. She just stared down at the truck. Pa had given it to her for her fifth birthday.

Ma saw me standing in the living room and came in wiping her hands on a towel.

"Jake," she said, "sit down. I need to tell you and Molly something very important."

"Is it about Pa?" Molly asked.

I wanted to tell Ma that I already knew he was dead. I wanted to save her the pain of having to tell us the news, and me the pain of having to hear it again. But I didn't want her to know I had been spying on her last night, so I just sat there quietly.

"Yes," Ma began, "it's about your father."

She paused for a minute. I could tell that she was searching for the right words to say. It was like she'd had everything all thought out beforehand, but now, when it came to actually telling us, she wasn't sure how to put it into words. She took a deep breath and closed her eyes. "Your Pa has… has gone to be with Jesus. And I'm afraid we won't see him again, down here on earth."

I didn't say anything. I knew this explanation was more for Molly's sake than mine. They were always so careful about what they'd say around her. Like when our dog, Chief, had gotten hit by a car the summer before, and they were so worried about how upset she'd be. I remembered being angry because it seemed like they were more concerned about her feelings than mine.

"You mean Pa's up in heaven?" Molly said.

Ma nodded. "Yes dear, he's up in heaven with Jesus. And he's very happy."

"Didn't he like it down here. Didn't he like us no more?"

"No, honey." Ma clutched Molly's hand. "No, he loved us very much—"

"Then why did he want to leave?"

Ma looked confused and started to sound muddled. “Well… he—he didn’t *want* to leave…”

She was so concerned about getting Molly to understand Pa’s death that she didn’t even realize how mixed up things were at this point. And it was her own fault. I have to confess, I almost laughed at her. It served her right.

“You mean Pa didn’t *want* to go to heaven?” Molly persisted.

“Yes—I mean no,” Ma said. “Well, he… he didn’t really have a choice—”

“Did Jesus *make* him go?”

At that point something inside of me burst. I was tired of listening to my mother trying to candy-coat her explanation. I was tired of Molly’s feelings always being placed above my own.

“Oh for crying out loud, Molly, Pa’s *dead!*” I shouted. “And he ain’t ever coming back!”

“*Jake*!” Ma shrieked, looking horrified.

But I didn’t care. I stood up and started to shout louder. “He got killed by an alligator plain and simple! He didn’t *have* no choice. It dragged him under the water and it *killed* him! You get it? It *killed* him!”

Ma looked so shocked, she couldn’t even move. She just stared at me with her mouth open. Molly glared at me in disbelief. Her eyes were fierce for a moment, but then started to fill with tears and her lower lip began to quiver.

But I was too angry to care.

I ran outside, slamming the door behind me. At that moment I wanted to run as far away from both of them as I could. I wanted to start my life all over again with a whole new family. I wanted to forget that I’d ever had a mother and sister. What was the point? It was useless to go on trying to be a family anymore without Pa. We would never be the same again.

I ran through the field, back to the river where Buck and I always sat. I threw myself down on the grassy bank and lay there for a long while staring up at the sky. The morning dew soaked through my shirt but I didn't care. A part of me wanted to get as far away from home, and Silas, and everything here that I had ever known. Part of me never wanted to see any of them ever again. But part of me wanted to hold onto them as tight as I could.

12

I don't know how long I laid there. It was most of the morning. By the time my hunger pangs convinced me to go back the sun was nearly straight overhead. When I returned, I saw a big blue car with Georgia license plates parked in the driveway.

It was Ma's sister Lola and her husband Buddy. They had driven all night from Atlanta.

Ma didn't have any other family. Both of her parents were dead, and it was just Ma and her older sister left. I had always known Aunt Lola as a tall woman with stiff hair and lots of makeup. She apparently enjoyed dressing up when they were kids while Ma just wanted to play sports. Lola had moved up to Atlanta after high school to study clothing design or some such. She met Buddy shortly afterward. Buddy Sullivan was a photographer who took pictures for clothing catalogues. He was short and chubby, and always wore plaid sport coats and sunglasses and called everyone 'Sport'. He was pretty much bald except for a few strands of hair that he plastered across his scalp.

He and Aunt Lola got married. Of course, this was all before I was even born. Buddy and Lola never had kids of their own, and now they were in their forties. They liked to travel and eat out, and I guess they thought having kids would've interfered with all that. They'd come to visit at Christmas time, and we'd go to see them once every couple of years during the summer.

They had a very big house with lots of fancy little things that break easily. I never enjoyed those visits because I usually had to sit very still in the living room and listen to Lola and Buddy talk about themselves. To be honest, I don't think Pa had ever enjoyed it either.

I snuck into the kitchen and could hear voices in the livingroom. I figured if I could make a sandwich very quietly and sneak up the back stairway, they wouldn't know I had come in. I never got past slicing the bread.

"Jake," Ma called, "come here and say hi to Aunt Lola and Uncle Buddy."

I cringed and walked into the livingroom.

Ma and Aunt Lola were sitting on the sofa, and Buddy sat across from them in Pa's easy-chair. Molly sat on the floor beside her truck. Aunt Lola motioned to me. Her hair was all up in a scarf, and she didn't have any fancy clothes on because they had driven all night. I could tell that she'd been crying because her eyes had black rings underneath. Her lipstick was as bright red as the purse that she clutched on her lap.

I reached out to shake her hand.

"Oh Jacob, honey." She opened her arms and smothered me with a bear hug. The smell of her perfume was so thick, it almost made me gag. She sobbed against my cheek and I could feel her hot breath on my neck. Then she stood me up and looked at me, dabbing her eyes with a tissue.

"My, you've grown this last year." She blew her nose. "We've missed you all very much."

She spun me around and sent me over to Buddy who reached out a soft, meaty hand and grabbed hold of mine.

"How ya doin', Sport?"

"Okay," I mumbled, wanting to leave.

He ruffled my hair. "Good to see you, kiddo."

For a while nobody said anything. The only sound was the slow ticking of the grandfather clock in the corner. Molly just gave me an icy stare.

"Can I make myself a sandwich?" I asked.

Ma nodded and looked down. I couldn't tell if she was angry with me, or sad or what.

"Sure, go ahead."

I breathed a sigh of relief and went back to the kitchen. I made myself a sandwich and took it upstairs to my room. The window was open and I climbed out onto the porch roof. We had a big oak tree in the front yard that kept this part of the roof in the shade most of the day. Sometimes Buck would come over at night and climb the tree onto the roof and tap on my window. We'd sit out there for hours some nights.

Just as I finished my sandwich, another car pulled up the driveway. It was Yancey and Clara Buckman, probably just coming from church.

"Come in," I heard Ma say when they knocked on the front door.

I went back inside to hear what was going on. I sat on the stairway and listened.

"We were all so shocked when we heard," Mrs. Buckman was saying through her tears.

Yancey told her that the whole church had held a special prayer meeting for us after the morning service. He said they were going to take up a collection to help with the funeral expenses and anything else we might need. I could hear Ma's voice crack as she thanked them.

Then I heard Yancey ask about me.

"How's young Jake taking this?"

"It must've been horrible for him to see that," Mrs. Buckman sobbed, "just horrible."

Ma didn't answer them right away. She paused so long that I knew she must've been crying. I moved down a step to hear better. She was talking very softly.

"I don't know what's gotten into him," I heard her say. "He just seems so angry. He yelled at poor Molly this morning when I tried to tell them…"

She started to cry. It was very quiet for a while and all I could hear was Ma sobbing softly. After a minute, she spoke again.

"He ran outside and was gone all morning. Molly was so upset… I didn't know what to do… or say. He just seems like an entirely different person."

"We know a doctor," I heard Aunt Lola say. "He's a specialist. He deals with children who've been through traumatic events like this. He's a member of the club—you know him Buddy, Joe Zemicki. He's really wonderful. Why when I—"

"Oh, I don't know if Jake needs a doctor," Ma said. "I just think he needs some time to adjust to all this. I don't even know if our insurance would—"

"Now don't you worry about that Ann, honey," Aunt Lola said. "Buddy can talk to him and we can help with your expenses. Don't you worry about a thing."

"Thanks Lola," Ma said. "Let's see how he does over the next couple days."

"Sure dear," Aunt Lola said. "We'll see how he does."

I almost started chuckling in spite of myself. If Aunt Lola had her way, the whole country would have to see a therapist. I was glad at least that Ma wasn't too quick to follow her idea.

All that afternoon folks called Ma to express their sympathy and dropped by for short visits. They brought casseroles and other dishes over so that Ma wouldn't have to concern herself with cooking. In fact there was hardly any room in the refrigerator to keep them all so Buddy helped himself to some of them. A lot of folks from church came by and that seemed to cheer Ma up a little.

At one point someone started telling stories about Pa and all the trouble he'd gotten into when he was younger. He had come from a poor family up in Comstock. His father had run out on his mother and him when he was ten, and they both had to work hard to make ends meet. His mother died when he was eighteen so Pa ended up getting in with the wrong crowd. He used to smoke and drink and cuss, and cause all sorts of trouble.

Then, when he was about twenty, he met Ann Marie Tyler. Ma had been raised by strict, God-fearing parents who went to church regularly and didn't take to Pa very well at all. But Pa was just crazy about their daughter. He used to ride his motorcycle over to their house and ask if he could take Ma out on dates. Her father would never give her permission to go, so Ma would sometimes sneak out at night, and they'd go out riding and dancing and such. They were both pretty rebellious at one time. I even heard Ma laughing a little at some of those stories.

Then, one day they were out riding on Pa's motorcycle and he hit a slick spot in the road. Ma was thrown off the bike and was in a coma for several days. It was during that time that Pa went through the biggest change of his life. He realized then that he'd been living for himself his whole life, and the only thing he'd ever wanted to do was have fun. But now his recklessness had nearly taken the life of someone he loved, and the guilt of it had broken his heart.

He figured that Ma's folks would hate him for what he'd done. They found him one night at the hospital, sleeping at Ma's bedside. To his surprise they hugged him and told him that they had forgiven him, and they weren't hateful at all.

That sort of thing was new to Pa, and I guess it must've made quite an impression. He'd caused them so much pain, yet they told him that they forgave him. They said they knew their daughter's life was in God's hands, and they knew they had to trust Him.

That kind of trust, they said, doesn't come when things are going smooth, but when it seems so dark you don't know which way to turn next. But they also knew that God understood exactly what they were going through because He once had to stand by and watch His only child die.

Pa had never seen that kind of faith in his whole life. He wanted to know how they could not be bitter at what he'd done. They had their Bible with them and started to read some passages, and before Pa knew what had hit him, he was crying like a baby.

All his years of being bitter and angry just melted away, and Pa talked to God for the first time in his life. He used to say that was the night he finally knew what it was like to be forgiven. That was the night he had become a whole new person.

Not too many days later, Ma came out of her coma. She said when she first saw Pa, he had shaved off his beard, trimmed his hair, and was holding a ring in his hand.

"Ann," he said, "I love you more than I can even describe. Will you be my wife?"

"I guess so," Ma answered, groggily. "But I don't think my boyfriend is gonna like it."

I sat alone on the stairs, listening to the stories people had to tell. I never knew how highly folks had thought of Pa. But none of it seemed very real. It was as if I was listening to stories about someone else I didn't even know. Part of me longed to go down and join them. But another part of me just wanted to be alone.

13

Shortly after supper, everyone had gone, and Ma, Aunt Lola, and Buddy were sitting on the front porch while Molly played in the yard. I had finally decided to come out and hunker down on the front steps. No one said anything. In the distance a dog barked, and somewhere a mourning dove cooed. The late afternoon sun blazed down, and a humid breeze ruffled the trees. I realized that it'd only been one day since Pa had died.

Twenty-four hours before, we were playing catch…

And it still didn't seem real to me.

Just then, the sheriff's truck turned up the driveway. Rooster was driving, and I could see that someone other than Billy Ray was sitting in the passenger seat. When they got out, I saw it was Ellis Woods.

They came up to the porch and Rooster tipped his hat. "Afternoon, Ann."

"Hello, Rooster," Ma replied, quietly. "You remember my sister Lola and her husband Buddy. They've come down from Atlanta."

"Oh, yes," Rooster smiled and tipped his hat again. "How d'ya do."

Aunt Lola nodded politely and fanned herself while Buddy waved and dabbed the sweat off his forehead.

Rooster looked down at his feet for a moment. "Well Ann, we've been out searching for this gator all day but we ain't seen a trace of it."

"You ain't givin' up already, are you Sheriff?" Buddy asked, scratching his stomach.

"Nooo," Rooster smiled and shook his head. "No sir. But Mr. Woods here has kindly offered his services to help us track this thing down."

"That's mighty kind of you Mr. Woods," Ma said.

Ellis just smiled and nodded.

Rooster cleared his throat and continued. "The thing is, Mr. Woods has got… well a different sort of way of trackin' this thing, and I just thought you should know what's going on."

Ma frowned. "What do you mean *different sort of way*?"

At that point Ellis spoke up. "Well, like I told the Sheriff here, all these boats out on the river are doing more harm than they are good."

"How's that?" Buddy raised one eyebrow. He pulled out another handkerchief to wipe his forehead and neck.

"See, all the noise and commotion they're making tends to drive wildlife farther away. Now this gator may have had that part of the riverbank staked out for a nest.

That might explain why it was so aggressive toward your husband. All this activity might drive it down river or deeper into the swamp. But if things quiet down a bit, it may decide to come back."

Buddy just grunted skeptically and popped open a bottle of root beer.

"Now what I've asked the sheriff," Ellis went on, "is to give me two or three days to search for this alligator alone. I'm pretty confident that I can find it."

"You mean call off the search?" Buddy scowled. "That thing could be miles away in two or three days if you don't find it on your own fella."

Ellis rubbed his eyes. I could tell that Buddy was starting to irritate him. "Look, I've worked around these animals for twenty years. I've come to know their general habits very well. I can track this one down. I just need some time."

Ma narrowed her eyes and studied Ellis for a moment. "You're the one who found the gator that killed that little girl up in Chase this spring?"

Ellis looked down. "Yes," he said softly. "Yes ma'am, I did."

"You found it by yourself?"

"Yes ma'am."

Ma turned back to Rooster. "What do you think?"

Rooster shrugged. "I think we could spare three days. Most of them folks out searchin' knew Jack pretty well. I'm sure they'd just as soon stay out there and find that gator, but I'd like to give 'em time to attend Jack's funeral and grieve properly."

Ma nodded. "I understand."

"If he can't find it in three days, we'll start the search up again," Rooster said.

Buddy grunted once more and muttered, "In three days, that gator'll have made it to the Gulf."

Ma offered them sodas but Rooster declined and as they turned to leave, I stood up.

"Mr. Woods, I'd like to come with you. I'd like to help you find that gator."

I heard Aunt Lola gasp.

"No, Jake," Ma said, sternly.

Ellis scratched his head. "I understand how you feel," he said. "But I'm afraid I can't take you with me."

"Please," I persisted. "*Please*. I promise I won't get in your way—"

"Jake," Rooster said. "You're the man of the house now. That's a big responsibility. And right now your Ma needs you here."

I knew I was fighting a losing battle and I wasn't about to go on begging. Ma didn't need me here. She had Aunt Lola and Buddy to help her with everything. I could tell he was trying to make me feel like I was important, but I knew it was just a trick to get me to forget about going with Ellis. I felt my hands tightening into fists and my jaw clenching. Then I felt a hand on my shoulder. I looked up and saw Ellis smiling down at me.

"I know how badly you want to help me find this thing, Jake," he said, softly. "But I promise you'll be the first to know when I do."

I just looked down and didn't say a word. Ellis patted my shoulder again, and then he and Rooster got back into the truck. As they drove away, the silence that had surrounded us before returned again.

14

The next few days were the longest ones I had ever experienced in my life. Ma and Aunt Lola had spent most of the time making arrangements for the funeral which they had planned for Wednesday.

On Monday morning I got up early, packed myself a lunch, and went into town. I spent the whole day sitting on the dock down by the hardware store, just staring out at the river. I don't know exactly what I was hoping to see. I guess I hoped Ellis Woods would come around the bend in his boat, towing the big carcass of that alligator. But he never did.

I had thought about finding Buck so that at least I'd have someone to talk to, but deep down I wasn't sure if I felt like having company just yet. The last time I had seen him, he was sitting in the back seat of Frank Bussie's car, just staring straight ahead.

Part of me felt bad for him and wanted to call him right away, but another part didn't have much interest in doing all the things we used to do. It was as if two voices were fighting for my attention, and right now the part of me that wanted to be alone was starting to win.

Molly on the other hand, soon began playing in the dirt again, though she had stopped using the truck Pa had gotten her for her birthday. She brought it with her everywhere she went, but never got it dirty.

When I woke up Wednesday morning, I could tell it was going to be one of those blistering, hot days when there's not even a breeze blowing. The air was so thick with humidity, it seemed to hang on you and weigh you down like a wet blanket.

I came downstairs, dressed in my good Sunday clothes, with my cotton shirt sticking to my back and arms, and a tie that felt like it was strangling me.

Ma was in the livingroom, wearing a black dress that I had never seen before. She was brushing Molly's hair. Molly had on her Sunday dress as well with a big red bow that tied in the back.

I sighed and slumped into one of the chairs. "Do I *have* to go?"

Ma stopped brushing Molly's hair and put her hand under my chin. "I'd sure appreciate it if you did."

"But I really don't feel like it. It's gonna be awful hot."

She gave me a serious look. "Jake, I wish more than anything that I didn't have to go either. More than anything. But I need you to be there with me. Even though there's all these folks around, wishing us well, and sayin' nice things… well, the truth is right now, I feel like I'm all alone. I miss your father so much, and all the comforting words in the world don't seem to help. In fact, the only thing that brings me *any* comfort right now is just being with you and Molly."

I wanted to tell her that, deep down, I felt the same way. Even though lately I just wanted to be by myself, there was still a part of me that wanted to be with them no matter what.

I struggled to find the words to tell her, but before I knew it, the chance was gone.

Aunt Lola came bustling out of the spare bedroom, adjusting her skirt, and looking at her watch. "Well, look at the time, would you. It's almost ten o'clock and we ain't even out the door."

She herded us along with her. Outside, Buddy was waiting in the car with one arm out the window, drumming his fingers on the roof. I climbed into the big back seat with Molly and Ma, while Aunt Lola got in the front, pulling on her white gloves.

"Buddy, you remember how to get to the church, don't you?"

"Aw, for pete's sake," Buddy muttered. "There ain't but three streets in the whole town. It's not like we're gonna need a map."

Our church sat on a small lot right next to the school. It was just a simple, white building with a little steeple at one end. As we pulled up, I noticed a big black car parked outside. Ma said it was the hearse where they would put the coffin when it was time to drive over to the cemetery.

We walked up to the front doors, and I started to get nervous. The thought of seeing my father laying in a coffin was actually making me feel sick. Like two cats were fighting inside my stomach. It felt just like the time I had to be in the school play. I remembered standing backstage in a cold sweat, waiting to say my lines. Waiting for that night to be over.

As we entered the foyer of the church, I thought of running away and hiding out somewhere until the funeral was over, but I knew they'd send folks out to search for me, and that would just make things worse.

The whole inside of the church looked very different than it usually did on Sunday mornings. It was full of flowers and smelled like overly-sweet perfume. I felt like I was being hugged by Aunt Lola all over again, only this time I couldn't get away from it.

And at the front of the church, surrounded by flowers, was the big bronze colored coffin, closed up tight.

Sam Watson and his wife Fayette were already there. Sam was nearly eighty years, old but he still had most of his hair. Even though he never liked being called *pastor*, he was still the person most folks went to whenever they needed answers or advice about spiritual things. He was probably the one person in town, other than Ma, who had known Pa the best. He had performed their marriage ceremony and had even given Pa his first Bible.

Fayette Watson started playing soft, somber music on the organ. We all went up to the front and stood by the coffin.

I felt relieved that the casket was closed. I didn't want to see Pa's lifeless body. And yet it made me sick to think of what must've happened to him under the water. I wondered how badly he'd been torn up for them not to leave the casket open. I wondered how long it had taken him to die. Did it happen quickly? Or did he suffer long while being twisted and shaken?

I could feel my hands growing moist and cold with those thoughts. I knew I shouldn't even be entertaining such things.

My thoughts were interrupted as Aunt Lola started wailing and sniffling. She made such a fuss that Buddy had put his arm around her and walk her to the back of the church. Just a few minutes before, she had scolded him for his wrinkled trousers and for not parking in the right spot. But now she was all sorrowful and teary-eyed.

Ma didn't have any expression on her face at all. She stared at the casket, but it didn't seem like she really *saw* it. She reached out her hand and touched the shiny metal edge. She didn't say a word and her lip didn't quiver, but I could see a tear swell up in her eye and roll gently down her cheek, leaving a little trail behind it like a tiny, melancholy river.

After a long while, she spoke. "All right, you kids can go sit down."

Then she went back and talked to Sam for a few minutes. I took Molly over to sit down in the front pew. She didn't sit still for very long, and soon began to fidget. I scolded her to keep still but she just gave me a look like she knew a secret that I didn't know and she was going to rub it in some.

"Ma says that Pa's up in heaven," she said, rocking in the bench.

"Yeah, I know," I said, trying to ignore her.

"She says he's with Jesus."

"So what?"

I could tell she was watching me and she had a curious expression on her face.

"Are you mad at me?" she asked after a minute. She had never asked me *that* question before. Normally, she knew full well when I was mad at her.

"No, I ain't mad at you," I grunted.

She was quiet for a few seconds, and then asked, "You mad at Ma?"

I sighed. "No, I ain't mad at Ma neither."

"Well, who *are* you mad at?"

"I ain't mad at anyone. Now hush."

She was quiet for a little while longer. Then she sighed and shook her head. "You sure look mad."

I scowled at her. "You talk too much."

By that time, Ma, Aunt Lola, and Buddy came and sat down next to us. Soon, more folks began to arrive and the church started to get crowded.

By eleven o'clock, it looked like everyone in town had shown up, and then some. Most of the people who worked with Pa at the mill had come down from Chase. Even Rooster Mason and Billy Ray Martin had taken some time off to come by. They sat near the back, dressed in crisp freshly-pressed uniforms.

All the windows of the church were wide open, and they had brought in several electric fans all humming and clacking, trying to keep the air circulating. But still folks were fanning themselves with pamphlets and hymnals. The whole place was silent and somber.

Then Sam Watson got up and announced an opening hymn. Fayette accompanied on the organ while everyone sang, *'Tis so Sweet to Trust in Jesus.*

Afterward, Sam wiped his forehead with a handkerchief and said, "You know it's easy to be sad when a loved one passes on. We think about how much we'll miss them and how things will never be the same again. But the Bible tells us in no uncertain terms that death is not the end of us."

He opened up his old Bible and began to read. "Behold, I show you a mystery; we shall not all sleep, but we shall all be changed, in a moment, in the twinkling of an eye…"

I had heard this all a thousand times before. My folks had brought me to church my whole life, but now I was starting to wonder if it was really true at all. Now it all seemed different, like the words were meant for someone else but not for me.

"…for this corruptible must put on incorruption and this mortal must put on immortality…"

I wondered then: what if *nothing* happened to you when you died? What if you just disappeared and never saw or heard or felt anything ever again? All that was left of my father was soon to be dumped in the ground and covered over with dirt.

"…O death, where is thy sting? O grave, where is thy victory?"

How could they be so sure Pa was in heaven? How could they be sure of anything? Old Sam was reading with such confidence that he made it *sound* believable…

But how could he know for sure?

"…But thanks be to God, which giveth us the victory through our Lord Jesus Christ."

Sam went on with his sermon. He said some nice things about how good a man Pa was—so much so that I started feeling kind of proud. He talked about the kind of man Pa used to be and how God had come in and changed his life around. Then he talked about how we all needed to let God into our hearts to forgive us and change us as well.

There was a part of me that still wanted to believe everything he was saying. It believed all the stories I had been taught in Sunday School—that there was once a man who died and came back to life. A part of me believed. But deep inside, another part of me was starting to doubt.

But it felt like such a small part. And it only seemed to doubt a little…

15

After Sam finished we sang another hymn and then Yancey Buckman, Jolly Meyer, Frank Bussie, and three other men from the mill where Pa worked gathered around the casket and carried it out to the hearse. Ma and Molly and I got up and followed them with Aunt Lola and Buddy right behind us.

As we walked down the aisle, I noticed Buck Miller sitting in the last row. I almost didn't recognize him at first. His hair was combed neatly and he was wearing one of the shirts he had earned working for Pa. He was sitting all the way in the corner, looking down, almost as if he was asleep. Next to him was a thin pale woman wearing a plain blue dress, headscarf and dark glasses. She was also looking down.

It was his mother.

In all the years I had known Buck, I never recalled his mother ever coming to church. Ma had invited her plenty of times but she never accepted. Now here she was, hunched slightly forward, as if trying to make herself look smaller. Trying not to be noticed.

I waited for Buck look up, but he never did.

We followed the casket outside where two men in black suits helped guide it into the back of the hearse. Then they closed the tail gate, started the engine, and pulled out onto the road. We got back in Buddy's car and pulled up behind it.

One by one, the rest of the cars lined up behind us in single file. Rooster had washed and polished his sheriff's truck. He turned on the top lights and pulled in front of the hearse to lead the entire procession.

The whole line of cars, probably more than thirty of them all together, followed the sheriff out of town and up Highway 47 toward Comstock. We drove about five miles and turned off onto Blue Pine Road, which took us right up to the Cedar Grove Cemetery. We passed through a big iron gate and followed a narrow road through the beautiful wooded area, past hundreds of neatly-groomed graves, to the plot that Ma had picked out between two large oaks.

The whole line of cars stopped, and the pallbearers took the coffin over to the grave site. There were some chairs set up for us underneath one of the oaks and it was quite a bit cooler in the shade. A light breeze carried the scent of flowers and freshly-cut grass. After several minutes, everyone had gathered around. Sam gave another short message and then ended the funeral with a prayer.

"Lord, we ask you to comfort Ann Marie and the children. Be with them during this difficult time, and fill them with peace; the peace of knowing that Jack is with you, and that one day they will see him again. Amen."

We sang one last hymn. It was soft and slightly out of tune, and a lot of folks were crying and sniffling. Ma didn't sing at all though. She just stared down at the casket.

Gradually, folks started to leave. They stopped by to express their sympathy to Ma and she wiped her eyes and thanked them politely. I searched through the crowd, but I didn't see Buck or his mother again.

After everyone had gone, we found ourselves alone beside the grave. Even Aunt Lola and Buddy had gone back to the car to wait for us. Ma took Molly onto her lap and put her arm around my neck to pull me close. She hugged us both and all I could think of was what she had said earlier about how the only comfort she had these days was being with me and Molly.

"Is Pa really inside there?" Molly asked, pointing to the casket.

Ma looked thoughtful for a moment.

"No," she said, "no, your Pa's with Jesus up in heaven. What's inside that coffin is just the stuff that's left over when we die. Sort of like when a caterpillar changes into a butterfly and leaves its cocoon behind."

Somewhere in the trees, a mourning dove cooed softly. We stayed there for a few minutes longer. Finally, Ma gave a long sigh and said that it was time to go.

But I didn't want to leave. A couple of hours before, I didn't even want to come to this funeral, and now I didn't want to leave. I wasn't ready to go yet. The casket had been closed during the whole funeral, and we hadn't even been able to see Pa one last time. He was inside that coffin and soon they would put him in the ground and cover him over with dirt. It seemed like we were ready to go on a long trip and were just going to leave him behind. Even after all the things Ma had told us and the things old Sam had read out of the Bible, I felt sure that I was never going to see Pa again.

And I didn't want to go.

I felt a gentle tug at my shoulder. And in spite of how much I wanted to stay, I felt myself walking away, following my mother as she carried Molly back to the car. But I kept looking back at the bronze-colored coffin between the two trees surrounded by flowers.

"G'bye Pa," Molly said softly, resting her chin on Ma's shoulder.

We drove back to the church in silence. They had planned to serve lunch and visit together after the funeral. We had ham sandwiches, potato salad, and punch.

Before long, folks were talking and laughing and carrying on. It was as if they'd forgotten all about the funeral just a couple hours before.

Aunt Lola was busy talking with several folks, telling them all about Atlanta and all the interesting and famous people she'd gotten to know. Buddy was helping himself to his third sandwich and seconds on potato salad.

Even Ma had seemed to forget about how sad she'd been earlier. She laughed and talked with Lenora Delwicky and Mrs. Buckman.

I wasn't in much of a mood to talk to anyone—or to listen to anyone for that matter, so I decided to go outside. There was a big tree in the back of the church with an old wooden swing hanging from one of its branches. It wasn't very comfortable, but at least there wasn't anyone else around, so I sat there for a while. After several minutes, I heard voices coming from the parking lot on the other side of a row of tall bushes. They were speaking in hushed tones but I could still hear what they were saying.

"…it was pretty bad," said one voice. "I hear even Doc Graham was shook up. Said he'd never seen anything like it in his life."

"No kidding?" said the other voice.

"He said Jack was tore up so bad, he couldn't even recognize him at all."

"I never heard of anyone being attacked that bad before."

"Well, that fella from Bilford was there too—that alligator fella. He said, judgin' by the teeth marks, it was a real big gator. At least ten feet."

The other man whistled.

"Yeah," the first man said. "And his boy saw the whole thing. Can you imagine that? A boy having to watch his Pa get killed like that?"

"You gotta wonder what that's done to his head."

Then the two men, smoking cigarettes, came around the edge of the bushes. The first man was Billy Ray Martin, all dressed up in his deputy uniform. The other man was tall and husky, with shaggy brown hair and a thick mustache. After a moment, I recognized him. It was Buck's father, Earl Miller. I didn't remember seeing him during the funeral and from the way he was dressed, it looked like he'd just gotten into town from one of his hauls.

They both looked surprised at first and then a little sheepish. I tried to ignore them and act like I hadn't heard anything they had said.

"Uh… hey, Jake," Billy Ray said. "How ya doin'?"

I just nodded. "Fine."

Earl Miller just looked away, pretending he had seen something off down the road.

They kept on walking and soon I was alone again. My hands gripped the ropes so tightly, my knuckles started to hurt. I didn't know if I was angry at them or just in shock by what I had heard, but I started to feel sick inside again.

I don't think I spoke to anyone the rest of the day—not even Ma.

That night I layed awake in bed, staring at the ceiling. Billy Ray and Earl Miller's voices kept echoing in my head.

Jack was tore up so bad, he couldn't even recognize him.

His boy saw the whole thing.

You gotta wonder what that's done to his head.

I started to feel like nothing during the last several days had really happened at all. I felt as though my whole life had just been a dream, and I wasn't really the person I thought I had been. I kept thinking that soon I'd wake up and find myself in another bed, in another home with a completely different family.

16

It was close to midnight when I heard a soft tapping sound outside my window and a hushed voice.

"Jake. Hey Jake."

I peeked out and saw Buck crouched on the roof. For the first time since Pa had died, I actually felt glad to see someone.

"Hey Buck," I whispered and motioned him to come inside. There was suddenly such a rush of things I wanted to say to him that I didn't know where to begin. "How're ya doin?"

"Okay," Buck whispered as he climbed inside.

I sat on the edge of my bed and Buck slid a chair over. We just sat there, quiet for a while. I wasn't even sure where to start.

"Sorry for not calling or anything," I said, finally. "But I didn't—"

"Aaah, don't worry about it." Buck waved it off. "I figured you were… y'know, busy."

“Actually, I’ve been pretty bored the last few days.”

“Whaddaya mean?”

I shrugged. “The last couple of days I’ve been just sittin’ on the dock, waitin’ to see if they caught that gator.”

“I hear Ellis Woods is huntin’ for it by himself.”

“He came by with the sheriff on Sunday. He said he’d be able to track it down better if there weren’t so many boats out on the river.”

“Have you heard anything?” Buck asked.

“Nope. Sheriff said he’d give him three days to find it, then he’d send the boats back out again.”

Buck shook his head. “If he ain’t found it by now, no tellin’ where it might be.”

Then we both fell silent for a few minutes until Buck spoke again. This time his voice quivered slightly. “I’m… I’m sorry about your Pa. I still can’t believe he’s really…”

A breeze brushed back the curtains and the moonlight shown in on Buck’s face for a second. He looked like an old man sitting there, staring down at his feet, just like I had seen him earlier that day in church.

“Yeah, me neither,” I said. “I kind of feel like he’s just away on a trip somewhere, and he’ll be coming back in a few days.”

We listened to the wind pick up outside. It the shook branches of our oak and they scraped against the shingles.

“I saw you at the funeral today,” I said. “I tried to get your attention.”

Buck nodded. He had a faraway look in his eyes. "My Ma didn't want to go—she hates funerals. But I made her take me."

"I saw your dad at the church. After we got back from the cemetery."

Buck grunted. "He's been on the road since last Tuesday. He just got back this morning. I'm surprised he even showed up—although there was free food, I suppose."

I just shrugged. I didn't know what to say.

After a moment, Buck looked at me very seriously. "D'you believe all that stuff that guy was sayin' today—about God and all?"

I nodded. I didn't want to tell him I was having doubts myself. "Yeah, I guess so."

Buck shook his head. "I don't know. If there is a God, I don't think he knows what he's doin' sometimes. Either that, or he's real mean."

"Why's that?"

"It just don't seem fair that he'd let your dad die when there are so many other folks who deserve to get killed—and he lets them live."

"Whaddaya mean?"

Buck sighed. "Like my pa. He's hardly ever home. And when he is, he don't hardly say two words to me. It's like he doesn't even know I'm alive. Sometimes I really hate him."

Off in the distance, we could hear the quiet rumble of thunder. A storm was coming.

Buck got up and stared out the window. "It just don't seem fair. My old man couldn't care less about me. *He's* the one who shoulda got killed. Not your pa."

"Buck, don't talk like that." I couldn't believe what I was hearing. I had always known Buck wasn't very close with his father, but I never thought he *hated* him that much.

Thunder rumbled again, louder.

After a few seconds Buck turned around. "I should get going. I'll see ya tomorrow maybe, huh Jake?"

"Sure," I said, softly. "I'll see ya."

With that, Buck climbed back outside, down the tree and was gone.

I lay back down. That night, I had another dream. I was back at the church, standing in front of the casket, staring down at it. A voice kept echoing in my mind. *Jack was tore up so bad... he couldn't even recognize him... his boy saw the whole thing.*

I touched the casket lid. It felt like ice—so cold it almost burned. I pulled back my hand, but something made me try again. I grabbed a cloth to protect my hand and then slowly opened the lid…

It was empty.

The next thing I knew, I was in a boat on the river, surrounded by darkness and a dense fog. I didn't have any oars, and was just drifting along with the current until I felt the boat bumped into something under the surface. Then I realized I wasn't in a boat at all. I was inside the coffin, floating down the river. I heard a second bump and peeked over the side but couldn't see anything on the water.

Suddenly, a hand shot up from under the water and grabbed hold of my wrist. I tried to scream, but then Pa's head broke through the surface. He clung to me desperately, choking and gasping for air!

"Help!" he rasped. "Help me Jake!"

I pulled as hard as I could. The coffin nearly capsized as he tried to climb inside, but he couldn't quite make it. I wasn't strong enough.

"Help me, Jake! It's coming! It's behind—"

The next thing I knew, a giant black shape rose out up of the water. Yellow eyes burned through the fog. Huge jaws clamped down around Pa's chest and with one twist of its massive head, tore him loose from the coffin, loose from my grip, and yanked him back under the water.

A bright flash of light seemed to burn right through my eyelids, and a deafening clap of thunder woke me out of my nightmare. I sat up with a jolt in a cold sweat, my chest pounding. I was clutching my pillow and panting so hard, I felt like I had just run five miles.

The wind moaned and rain beat against my windows. Another flash of lightning lit up the sky, and for a second, I could see our oak tree bending in the wind. A moment later, a deep crash of thunder shook the whole house. I lay back down and tried to fall asleep again, but my heart was still pounding and I was still haunted by the visions of my dream.

17

I woke up the next morning to the sounds of Ma making breakfast down in the kitchen. Sunlight streamed into my room, and a fresh morning breeze blew warm air through my open window. I could hear Aunt Lola's voice over the clatter of dishes, though I couldn't make out what she was saying. I got dressed and went downstairs.

Ma had fixed scrambled eggs and toast, and I sat down to eat while she and Aunt Lola went into the other room. I could hear them talking in hushed tones.

"Atlanta's a good place to raise a family," Aunt Lola was saying. "And we'd be right there to help if you needed anything."

"I'm not ready to just pack up and move." Ma's voice was hardly above a whisper. "Jack and I worked hard on this place and I just can't leave it all behind."

"Ann honey, you've got to think about the kids. What'd be best for them?"

"I don't know. Right now I think we just need a little time to adjust."

I finished eating and went out to do my chores. I didn't think I could take listening to much more of their conversation.

Moving to Atlanta was the last thing I wanted to do. As if it wasn't a big enough shock to lose Pa, now Aunt Lola wanted us to move away from all our friends as well. I felt myself getting more and more angry at her. She had just moved right into our house and now she was trying to decide what was best for us. I paced around the barn with my frustration building up inside me. Even though Ma didn't sound like she was willing to move, I was still plenty worried. Aunt Lola could be pretty stubborn when she made up her mind about something.

Just then, I heard a car barrel up the driveway and skid to a halt on the gravel. I peeked out of the barn to see Frank Bussie getting out of his car.

"Ann," he called into the house. "Hey Ann!"

Ma came to the kitchen door. "What's wrong?"

"He killed it!" Frank said. "Ellis Woods killed the gator! He's got it down by the dock at the hardware store. I—I thought you might want to… to see it."

Ma turned pale at first, like she had seen a ghost. She looked as if she didn't know what to say. "Are you sure?"

Aunt Lola showed up in the doorway behind her with a look of disgust. "We don't want to see that thing. You just tell them to get rid of it."

Buddy's face appeared over her shoulder. He squeezed past them, out onto the doorstep still dressed in his white t-shirt and boxer shorts. The few strands of hair on his scalp waved around in the morning breeze.

"Nonsense," he grunted. "Of course we wanna see it—"

"Buddy!" Aunt Lola scolded him.

They started bickering and Frank was looking sorry he'd ever come by. Then Ma nodded. "I think we should go see it."

Aunt Lola stopped her bickering and gasped. "*What*?"

"Good," Buddy said. "Just let me get some clothes on and I'll…"

His voice trailed off as he disappeared back inside. Aunt Lola had a look of shock on her face. She shook her head. "Ann, you don't want to do this to yourself. It's not healthy. And what about the children?"

"You're right," Ma said. "You stay here with Molly. Jake and I will go."

Before Aunt Lola could recover or say anything else, Ma handed her the dish towel and was out the door.

"Tell Buddy we went with Frank," she said over her shoulder. "C'mon Jake."

We drove with Frank into town. There was a crowd of people gathered at the dock behind the hardware store. Frank tooted his horn as we pulled up and the crowd parted to let us through. As they did, I caught a glimpse of the carcass stretched out on the dock. It was big… even bigger than old Brutus. It had already been gutted and its pale belly was just an empty cavity.

Rooster Mason and Ellis Woods were standing next to it, talking together. The crowd was gaping and chattering with each other and some folks were snapping pictures. Ma and I walked out onto the dock and everyone got quiet as we drew up. I didn't notice them though, I was staring at the gator, tilting my head one way, then the other.

Rooster and Ellis came up to us and started talking to Ma. "It's almost thirteen feet long," Rooster said. "Biggest one we ever seen in these parts. Ellis here finally got it last night, right out where—er… right near that same spot at the park."

"Are… are you sure it's the one?" Ma said.

"Yes ma'am," Ellis nodded down at the animal. "This is the one all right."

"How do you know?"

There was silence for a moment. I saw Ma go off a ways to talk with Rooster and Ellis privately. But I couldn't take my eyes off the massive carcass. Flies swarmed around and it had an awful stench. The memory came back to me and I saw it rising up again out of the mud and reeds and ramming into my father like a freight train.

But something wasn't right.

Somewhere in the back of my head, a thought nagged at me. Soft and quiet, as if waiting for me to notice it. It whispered like my father's haunting voice in my dreams, growing louder and stronger, until it passed through my lips as a whisper…

"That's not it."

At first I thought it was my imagination, but as I closed my eyes, I could picture every detail. Every inch of it's armored hide. Every tooth in it's massive jaws. And when I opened my eyes again, I was sure.

It was just too small. The gator that killed Pa had made him look like a child in its jaws. This dead gator was big, but it wasn't as big as the one that had killed Pa.

It wasn't nearly as big.

Folks chattered around me, talking about how big this gator was, and how they felt safer now that it was dead. I looked around and shook my head. None of them had even seen the gator that killed my father. If they had, they'd have known this wasn't the same one. The *real* gator was still out there somewhere. It was still alive.

I went over to where Ma was talking with Rooster and Ellis.

"That ain't it," I said, pointing back at the carcass. "That ain't the one."

At first the three of them just stared at me with blank expressions. Then Rooster scratched the back of his neck and gave an uncomfortable chuckle. "Uh... how's that?"

"That ain't the gator that killed my pa," I said.

Ma blinked and shook her head. She opened her mouth like she wanted to say something but no words came out. Rooster and Ellis looked at each other and then back at me.

"And what makes you say that?" Rooster said.

"It ain't nearly big enough."

"Not *big* enough?" Ellis exclaimed, and then lowered his voice when Rooster hushed him. "What do you mean *not big enough*?"

I shrugged. "The one that killed my pa was a lot bigger. Maybe twice this size."

"*Twice the size?*" Ellis rubbed his eyes and pointed to the carcass. "That alligator is over twelve feet long. I can assure you it's fully capable of killing a grown man. Now, I know it might have *looked* bigger to you when you saw it in the water but sometimes things just *seem* bigger than they really are."

I turned to Ma. "You believe me, don't you?"

"Jake..." Ma said. "Please listen—"

"I know what I saw." I could hear my voice rising but I didn't care anymore. "None of you were even there—how can you tell *me* how big it was!"

Rooster put his hands up and glanced at the people behind me. "Now Jake, there's no need to get excited."

He tried to put his arm around my shoulder but I pulled away. I could tell they weren't going to believe me no matter what I said. It seemed the more I tried to convince them, the more they thought I was imagining things. I started to get furious.

"I *know* what I *saw*!" I said, as loud as I could. "And I'm telling you, the gator that killed my father is still out there somewhere!"

With that, I stomped off. I didn't know quite where I was going, I just knew I had to get as far away as I could. I heard folks muttering as I pushed through the crowd.

"What'd he say?"

"He said this ain't the gator what killed his pa."

"He said it was even bigger."

"Bigger'n this'un? Naw!"

Ma called after me.

"I'm goin' home!" I shouted over my shoulder. I didn't want to ride back home with her and Frank, and listen to them try to convince me that I was wrong and how my imagination had gotten the better of me. None of them had seen the attack. They didn't know how big the alligator was. And it was quite clear they would never believe me.

I cut across the vacant lot next to the hardware store where a trail followed along the river a ways. It met up with the road again at the bridge near our house. I'd sometimes take it as a shortcut home from school. I trudged along, scowling and muttering to myself, and kicking at the rocks along the path.

Halfway to the bridge, I passed an old rowboat tied up between two big oaks along the shoreline. I didn't think anything of it at the moment, I was too busy stewing over everything that had just happened. I turned around to see if anyone was following me, but Ma was still talking with Rooster and Ellis. Everyone else was gathered at the dock, pointing and making a fuss over the dead gator.

It was right then I heard a soft, deep voice come from the trees along the river.

"That ain't the one, is it?"

The voice sounded so quiet and calm, but gave me such a start, I nearly jumped out of my shoes. I saw a figure sitting on a large rock in the shadow of one of the trees. He'd been sitting so still that I would've walked right past him if he hadn't said anything. I couldn't quite tell who it was until he stood up and stepped out into the sunlight

It was Abraham Garner.

18

He wore the same faded overalls and straw hat as when I had seen him the week before. His coffee-black skin was creased and weathered like a worn-out leather boot, and his brown eyes were round and misty. There was a gentle look in them—not at all what I had expected to see up close like that.

He had a pipe clamped between his teeth and drew in a deep puff, blowing out the smoke from the corner of his mouth. Then he nodded over toward the dock. "That ain't the g-gator what killed your pa, is it?"

I stared at him for several seconds, too dumbfounded to speak. Even though I had seen him around town many times, I had never actually *talked* to him before. I guess I had never gotten up the courage. It had always been easier just to talk *about* him.

"No sir," I said. "You heard what happened?"

Abe blinked and then smiled. "It was in the n-newspaper." He looked down at me with one eyebrow raised. "I c-can read pretty fair y'know. P-pretty fair."

Then it dawned on me what he had said. He knew that the gator over on the dock wasn't the same one that had killed my father! He *knew*!

My eyes widened. "Wait! How do you know that ain't the one?"

Abe leaned forward and put a thick forefinger up, under his left eye. "Because I seen it."

I blinked and shook my head. "You *saw* it? Where? When?" My mind reeled with a million questions.

Abe point a thumb over his shoulder. "Out in the sw-swamp," he gunted and wagged his head. "Ain't like n-no other gator I ever seen n-n-neither." He nodded over to the dock and frowned. "N-nearly twice the size of that one."

"That's what I told them!" I blurted out. I could hardly contain myself. "But no one'll believe me. They won't even listen—not even Ma."

Abe turned and sat back down on his rock. "I d-don't reckon I'd believe it myself, if I hadn't see it with my own eyes."

My mind raced. Now that I had another eyewitness, I could convince Rooster and the others. They had to keep the search going. If I could just get old Abe to tell them what he'd seen, then maybe…

My heart sank. They wouldn't believe him either. As far as Rooster and most everyone else were concerned, Abe Garner was just a crazy old hermit. They wouldn't take his word about anything. I looked back at the dock and bit my cheek. There had to be another way.

"Where'd you see it?" I asked after a moment.

Abe took another long puff on his pipe. "Out in the d-deep swamp." He nodded down the river. "I was fishing a few weeks back and c-come up on the old boathouse. Saw him lyin' on the bank in the m-mud just sunnin' hisself." He grunted and shook his head. "Looked just like big log at first—like a tree had f-fallen over in the m-m-mud. Then I saw him move." His eyes widened. "Ssshh*eee*ww! He musta been over twenny feet long! Disappeared into the water. I seen him a c-couple times since then too, when he's comin' or goin'. Ain't like n-no other gator I ever seen though… n-no sir."

I looked at him sideways. "What do you mean *coming or going*?"

Abe shrugged. "I seen him swimmin' p-past my place a few times. Looked like he was headed out into the m-main river. I stayed p-pretty well clear of him though. Pretty well."

"When was the last time you saw it?"

Abe looked at me a moment and nodded, as if he understood. "Last Saturday m-morning."

What I said next came out so fast, I didn't even have a chance to stop myself. Before I knew what I was saying, I had already said it.

"Will you help me find it?"

It had taken me by surprise but Abe didn't seem the least bit startled. He shook his head. "Too dangerous. Whutch you gonna d-do when you find it?"

"Kill it."

"Kill it?" Abe laughed. "How you plan on k-killin' it?"

"We can shoot it," I said. "Ain't you got a gun?"

"C-course I gotta gun but I ain't gonna g-get a good shot at that beast. Not while he's in the water. We'd have to be too c-close. And he ain't d-dumb, this one. He ain't fat and slow. He's as quick as a p-p-panther—I ain't never seen a gator that quick before."

"Well maybe we could trap it?"

Abe gave me a suspicious look out of the corner of his eye. "How you g-gonna trap somethin' like'at? Lord, its like l-l-leviathan hisself!"

"I don't know!" I huffed and threw my hands in the air. "But that gator killed my pa and it's gonna kill someone else before too long. Unless I can kill it first."

Abe rubbed his jaw and looked out at the river. "I s'pose if we could get him c-close enough to shore where I could get a fair shot. I s'pose we m-might be able to kill it that way… I s'pose."

I grinned and rubbed my hands. "Great. When can we get started?"

Abe chuckled and cast a glance back toward the dock. "I d-don't reckon your ma would be too keen on the idea of you c-comin' out to the swamp."

"Aw, she won't mind," I said. "She lets me go pretty much wherever I like."

"That so?" Abe grunted and stood up and untied his boat from the tree.

"Yes sir. She won't mind at all."

He pushed the boat back into the water and climbed inside. Grabbing hold of the oars, he tipped his hat as he drifted away from shore. "Well, I s'pose if you can find my place, and if your ma says it's okay, I guess I won't mind a b-bit of c-company some days."

He rowed away while I stood on the bank and watched him disappear around the bend. I still couldn't believe I had spent the last few minutes talking to old Abe Garner!

He didn't seem like a murderer or cannibal at all. In fact, he seemed as pleasant and ordinary as anyone else in Silas—maybe even more so. I shook my head and chuckled to myself. At that moment I had only one thought on my mind.

Wait until I tell Buck!

19

"What?" Buck stared at me in disbelief.

"Yep." I grinned and folded my arms. "Abe Garner—in the *flesh*."

I called Buck as soon as I got home and he was over practically before I had hung up the phone. We went into the barn where he sat on a bale of hay and listened as I told him what had happened.

He shook his head. "Whew! What'd he say?"

"He said he knew that gator Ellis Woods had found wasn't the one that had killed my pa."

"How'd he know *that?*"

"He says he's seen the real gator out in the swamp. And he says it was nearly twice as big as the one Ellis killed."

Buck looked skeptical. "Ain't no gator that big out in the swamp."

"I *saw* it Buck," I said. "No one else was even there. I'm tellin' you—it was *huge*."

"But gators don't even get that big."

I sighed and sat down next to him. "No one else believes me either—not Rooster, not Ellis. Not even my own mother. They think I'm exaggerating—or crazy. But I *know* what I *saw*."

Buck seemed to study my face, as if to see if I was really telling the truth. "Okay, let's say there really *is* a giant alligator out in the swamp. What d'you plan to do about it?"

I leaned close. "I'm gonna kill it."

"*What*?" Buck winced like I had punched him. "You're crazy! How're you ever gonna find it in the first place? Even if you do, how're you gonna kill it?"

"I asked Abe to help me," I said.

Buck nearly fell over. "You asked… you asked Abe Garner to help you kill it? *Abe Garner*?"

I nodded. "I don't think all those stories about him are true. He didn't seem like a murderer or a cannibal or anything like that at all. He was actually a pretty nice old man."

"Sure," Buck snorted. "Until he gets you out to his old shack. Then he'll probably—"

"Never mind that," I said. "Are you gonna help me or not?"

"No way."

I sighed again and looked down at my feet. "Buck, the sheriff's called off the hunt. What d'you think is gonna happen the next time that gator gets hungry? Someone else is gonna get killed. You want that on your conscience?"

"And what if *I* get killed while we're out hunting for it? You want that on *your* conscience?"

"We'll be fine," I said. "Abe's got a gun and we won't even be in the water."

Buck folded his arms. "Then it sounds like you don't even need me."

"I do too," I grunted. "I never expected the sheriff or anyone else to believe me. But I thought at least *you* would."

I knew that last line would do the trick. I could tell Buck was feeling guilty. He fussed and fidgeted, and all it took was another minute of me looking sorrowful before I had him convinced to take a ride out to old Abe's shack with me.

We decided not to waste any time. Ma still hadn't gotten back from town so we packed a lunch, told Aunt Lola we were going over to Buck's house, and then headed out on our bikes.

Now rumor had it that Abe Garner's cabin stood at the end of an old dirt road near the edge of the swamp. We followed Highway 47 for a few miles, and turned off on a gravel road that followed along the river. After another half a mile we spotted a narrow dirt road which was nothing more than a pair of muddy tractor ruts that snaked their way through the woods for a little ways more. We rode cautiously along the path, keeping a sharp look out. The trees grew pretty thick around us and looked more than a little spooky. I have to admit, I started to feel like maybe my idea wasn't so good after all.

After a while, we caught a glimpse of an old shack through the trees up ahead. It was a small log cabin, all patched-up and sagging, with a little porch along the front. A big woodpile stood next to the shack with a narrow path running from the front porch, down a slope to a little wooden dock at the river. I recognized the green wooden rowboat tied up to the dock. The paint was faded, chipped, and peeling. The whole place seemed deserted, not a soul in sight.

We set our bikes behind a tree and crept up to the shack as quietly as we could. Crouching down behind the woodpile, we listened for sounds inside but couldn't hear anything. We peered into one of the windows, but the glass was too crusty and smudged to see inside. I started to get a creepy feeling, like when you think you're being watched.

Then we heard a voice behind us. "I d-don't generally get m-many visitors. Generally."

We both nearly jumped out of our skins, and turned around to see a huge figure standing over us. It was Abe Garner with a large axe resting on his beefy shoulder. My first thought was to run, but I couldn't get my feet to move. So we both just stood there with my heart pounding like a horse at full gallop.

Abe leaned forward to inspect us a moment, and then he smiled. "I see you m-managed to find your way out here," he said. "Your Ma know where you are?"

"Ye… uh, well… no." I stammered.

Abe snorted. "I thought as much. Still, you boys showed a lot of c-courage comin' out here by yourselves. Most folks don't c-come within a m-mile of my place. Most folks."

"Well, you said you'd help me find that gator." I said.

Abe grunted. "Oh yeah… the alligator."

His expression darkened and he raised the axe up over his head. We braced ourselves, ready to be chopped into pieces. But instead Abe turned and brought the axehead down into one of the logs on the woodpile where it stuck tight.

"You two g-got names?" he asked.

"Uh… I'm Jake," I said, breathing a sigh of relief. "Jake Kelly. And this here's my friend, Buck Miller."

"Buck and Jacob." Abe nodded. He took off his hat and wiped his forehead and neck with a handkerchief. "I r-reckon you know my n-name already."

We both nodded and Abe stared down at me for a few seconds longer. I could see a twinge of emotion in his misty eyes. Like a bit of sadness, as if he'd remembered something just then, from a long time ago.

"Too b-b-bad what happened to your pa," he said, finally. "A boy shouldn't have to lose his pa at your age. N-not at your age."

With that, he turned and disappeared around the front of the cabin. Buck and I looked at each other for a moment and then followed him. We found him standing on the front porch with his hands on his hips, looking around.

"Mo!"

We heard a shuffling noise from inside the cabin and then the sound of heavy paws on wood as a big brown dog trotted out the door. It was tall and lanky, with huge paws and a thick tail that wagged stiffly like a broomstick. Its oversized ears flopped loose and its big brown eyes looked sad and dreary. Abe reached down and scratched the dog behind its ears.

"This here's Mo," he said.

Mo trotted over to us. He didn't bark or raise a fuss at all. He just sniffed us, leaving big wet blotches all over our hands. Then he trotted back to the porch and plopped down next to an old rocking chair.

Abe sat down also and began to rock slowly. He took out his pipe and lit it up, drawing in several deep puffs.

I glanced at Buck and he just raised an eyebrow. I don't think either of us felt quite as nervous anymore.

Buck scratched the back of his neck. "That's a fine lookin' dog."

Abe just nodded and puffed on his pipe. We sat in silence for a long while. Mo raised his head to yawn and layed it back down again. Finally I spoke up.

"Uh, Mr. Garner… when do you think we can start looking for that alligator."

"In d-due time," Abe said, and raised an eyebrow. "It's n-not gonna be easy."

Buck folded his arms. "Is that gator really as big as Jake says it is?"

Abe nodded. "Twenny-two, twenny-three feet, maybe even bigger."

"Shoot," Buck snorted. "Alligators don't even git that big."

Abe chuckled. "But you ain't seen it, now have you?"

Buck shrugged. "Well… no…"

"Then how do you know how b-big it ain't?"

"I just read that they don't git no bigger'n ten or twelve feet at the most."

Abe drew in a deep puff and shook his head. "Well, I know what I seen. And that alligator ain't like no other one I ever seen in my life. And I seen plenty of 'em."

Buck grunted and looked at me for a second. Then he turned back to Abe. "Why don't you show us then. I'd like to see it myself."

"You just lookin' for trouble is all," Abe grunted. "I r-reckon you'll find plenty of it too… I reckon."

Then I spoke up. "You said you might be able to get close enough for a clear shot."

Abe shook his head. "That's a long ways back into the swamp."

"Please," I said, now feeling desperate. If I couldn't get Abe to help me, I didn't see who else I would be able convince. "*Please*? You said you'd help me."

Abe stopped rocking for a moment. He sat there, holding his pipe with a faraway gaze in his eyes, like he'd had a few minutes before. Then he looked at me thoughtfully.

"All right," he said. "Next time I g-go fishin', I suppose we could take the boat back into the swamp and take a look—but it's g-gonna cost you something."

"Anything!" I said, eagerly.

Abe looked around. "Well, I been needin' some help 'round the place. I ain't able to do so much lately. There's windas here that need c-cleanin'. And there's p-paintin' to do and the yard n-needs rakin'. And ol' Mo here ain't had a bath in…"

He paused and frowned down at the dog. "Well, he ain't *had* a b-bath."

"Okay, okay," Buck said. "When're you goin' fishing next?"

Abe shrugged. "D-day or two. I ain't gonna g-guarantee nuthin' though. If we don't find that gator, we don't find it."

"Fine," I said. "We'll come back tomorrow and help you clean up around here. Then you take us with you the next time you go fishing. Deal?"

Abe took another puff on his pipe and nodded. "Deal."

And that ended our first visit to Abe Garner's shack out in the swamp. We rode back home that afternoon filled with excitement, but we decided it would be best not to tell anyone about our pact with Abe Garner. We figured nobody in Silas would understand.

I was starting to feel like we had all misjudged old Abe terribly. In an odd way, he reminded me of Pa, the way he had set things up so that we'd have to do some chores in exchange for his help. I felt pretty good about the whole bargain though. Sure, it was going to be a lot of work but it would be worth it.

I wanted nothing more in the world than to kill that alligator. Then everyone would see I was right.

20

By the time we got home, it was the middle of the afternoon and Ma had come back from town. She was standing by the kitchen door as we rode up the driveway.

"Jacob," she said, "come inside, I'd like to talk to you."

I could tell by her tone of voice that she was pretty upset. That, and she called me 'Jacob.' Buck knew better than to stick around, so he left without even asking about supper.

I knew Ma wanted to talk about what had happened that morning, but I didn't feel like discussing it anymore. There wasn't any point. I knew I wouldn't convince her, and I sure wasn't going to tell her how I had met Abe Garner, or about the bargain we had made with him. She'd *never* have approved of that.

I followed her into the living room. Aunt Lola was sitting on the sofa where she and Ma had obviously been talking before I got home. When she saw me, she got up and went into the kitchen. Ma had me sit down with her on the sofa. That was usually the place I would have to sit whenever she or Pa had one of their 'serious discussions' with me.

I sighed to myself and rolled my eyes. I hated these conversations. They always seemed to last forever—usually because I would end up arguing with them about something or other. It was a futile tactic, though an unconscious one. I would never win those arguments, and all I ever managed to do was stretch out the conversation longer than it needed to be.

So right then I decided I would just keep my mouth shut and let Ma say her piece. I wouldn't argue or fuss. I wouldn't even make eye-contact. I would just agree with whatever she said, or apologize, or say whatever I had to in order to get this over with as quickly as possible.

Ma sat down, took a deep breath, and closed her eyes for a moment. "Jake," she began. "First of all, I know we've all been through a very difficult time this week, and I'm sorry if I haven't taken the time to talk to you about everything that's happened. I know it must've been very hard for you to see your Pa—"

Her voice cracked. She closed her eyes and took another deep breath. "To see that terrible thing happen to your father. I got so busy with my own grief and planning the funeral and all, that I didn't even take the time to think of your feelings. I want you to know I'm very sorry for that."

She paused. I had been staring at my feet so I wouldn't have to look her in the face. But she paused for so long that I figured she was expecting me to say something. I glanced up and saw that she had an odd expression on her face—not angry or anything, but like she was trying to figure out what I was thinking. I imagined she was wondering why I'd been acting the way I had. Normally, it was easy for me to talk to her. Normally, we talked about everything. I never used to have any problem telling her what was on my mind, so I imagined she was wondering why I wasn't talking anymore.

I figured I should at least acknowledge her, so I shrugged. "That's okay."

She put her hand on my knee. "It's not okay. Jake, you've been acting so strange. I don't even think I saw you cry at all for your father. You don't seem to want to talk anymore, and you just seem so angry lately."

I felt hot pricks on the back of my neck. The temptation to give her an explanation was growing stronger. This plan was harder than I expected. I took a deep breath and mustered my resolve.

"Sorry," I mumbled.

"You don't have to be sorry," Ma said. "I just want to know why you're acting this way. Are you mad at me?"

Her eyes were getting misty around the edges. I looked away quickly. "No."

I could feel my jaw clenching. After what happened down at the dock, she still didn't understand why I might be a little angry? Couldn't she see why I had a *right* to be angry?

"Well, who are you mad at? The way you talked to me this morning… it sure seemed like you were mad—"

"Because no one believes me," I heard myself blurt out. I knew I wasn't sticking to my plan but I didn't care. I couldn't keep it bottled up anymore. "Everyone thinks that gator at the dock is the one that killed Pa—but it's *not*! I *saw* it—and no one even believes me!"

"But Jake, the sheriff and Mr. Woods are *sure* that they got the right one."

"How would *they* know? They didn't even *see* it!"

Ma fidgeted and then looked down. "Jake…" Her voice softened. "They're sure."

"How can they be?"

She paused and took another deep breath. "Because Mr. Woods said he cut open the alligator to examine its stomach contents…" She suddenly looked very pale. "And he found this."

She opened her hand and showed me an object that I recognized right away. It was the wristwatch she'd bought Pa for his birthday last year. He wore it all the time.

I just stared at it. She was holding it right there in front of me but it still didn't seem real.

"Now Jake," Ma said. "I know you don't believe it, but the sheriff and Mr. Woods are very sure that alligator *is* the right one."

I could hear her talking to me but it suddenly felt like she was far away, talking to someone else. I just sat there looking at Pa's watch, shaking my head. I couldn't think of anything to say.

For a moment, I considered telling her about my encounter with Abe that morning. He was the only other eyewitness. But still… she had Pa's watch, and I started to doubt myself. Could I have been wrong? I closed my eyes, and once more the image of my father in the jaws of that gator came back to me…

No! I knew what I had seen. I wasn't imagining things. That gator down at the dock wasn't nearly as big. But how had it gotten Pa's watch?

"That doesn't prove anything," I said, after a moment. "Some other gator could've come along and swallowed his watch and—"

Ma closed her eyes suddenly, like she'd just been slapped in the face. "Jake, stop it! Stop doing that!"

I blinked. "Doing what?"

She looked straight at me. I could tell she was angry, but I had no idea why. "Stop fighting me! Stop making everything so difficult!"

I just stared at her. I hadn't expected her to get so angry. Then I remembered that I wasn't supposed to be arguing with her. That wasn't my plan. I had to think quick. I needed some way to get my plan back on track.

"I—uh… I'm sorry," I said, trying my best to sound sincere. "It was probably just a mistake. Maybe that gator *was* the one—"

"*Stop it*!"

"What now?" I asked.

"Now you're patronizing me."

"I don't even know what that means."

She started to answer me, but then she stopped and closed her eyes. "It means," she said, evenly, "that you're just agreeing with me so that I'll leave you alone. But I know what you're trying to do and it's not going to work."

I realized I had definitely underestimated her. She was sharper than I had given her credit for. However, now I was in an even tougher situation. Now I had to try to patronize her out of thinking that I was patronizing her... without sounding like I was trying to patronize her.

My mind reeled. "Uhhh…"

"Jake." She put her hand on my knee. Her voice was soft. "If you don't want to talk to me right now, you don't have to. Just promise me that you won't shut me out of your life forever."

I almost couldn't believe what I had heard. There are times when a parent does something so unexpected that you just have to stop and wonder. She was letting me go. She wasn't going to make me sit here and have a long, uncomfortable discussion with her after all.

But I thought about what she had just said. Of course, I didn't want to shut her out of my life. Certainly not forever. I just didn't have the time right now to try to sort everything out. I had too many other things on my mind. But she had given me my opening—my chance to escape. It was right there for the taking...

Then I discovered something else as well. I was feeling guilty. Sure the conversation was over—which was what I wanted all along. But somehow my victory didn't feel as satisfying as I thought it would. And then it dawned on me. Had she done that on purpose? Had that been her plan all along? To let me go but make me feel guilty about it?

Was she that clever after all?

21

The next morning, I finished my chores early, and Buck and I got ready to go back to Abe's cabin. We packed a lunch and grabbed our fishing poles. I told Ma we were going fishing and that we'd be gone most of the day. That's how we normally spent our summers anyway so she didn't look like she suspected anything.

By nine o'clock we were on the road, headed through town. The sun was already hot and we could tell it was going to be another humid day.

As we rode up to Abe's cabin, old Mo came trotting out to greet us with his tail wagging. He sniffed our hands again as if that was his way of saying *hello* or something. Abe was washing out a plate and a frying pan under a big handpump in front of the cabin He looked up and nodded.

"Mornin' boys," he said. "You two sure g-got an early start."

He finished with his washing and went back inside to put the things away. We followed him onto the porch and peeked in the doorway. The whole cabin was no more than twenty feet across and pretty dark inside.

Then we heard Abe's voice from the shadows. "Come on in."

We entered cautiously, and looked around. The only light came in through the open doorway behind us. As my eyes adjusted to the dim lighting, I could see that the place was actually quite tidy for the amount of stuff that was jammed inside. There was an old pot-belly stove right in the middle of the room. I could smell bacon, coffee and the sweet aroma of maple syrup, and it reminded me of breakfasts at home.

Over in one corner was a bed with a sagging mattress and wool blanket. Next to the bed stood a milkcan with a cloth over it and a kerosene lamp on top. At the foot of the bed was what looked like a pirate's treasure chest, all locked up with an iron padlock.

On the other side of the room stood a small table and two wooden chairs. Another corner was closed off by a thick curtain and looked like Abe used it for a pantry because we could see shelves with some cans of food stacked up on them.

Three large barrels were lined up along the back wall. Each one had an assortment of knick-knacks and carved figures on them. Two windows along the front wall were covered up by thick curtains.

Abe pulled the curtains back and the whole room lit up brightly. I heard a gasp, and noticed Buck's face. He was staring over my shoulder at something. His eyes were round as saucers.

I turned to see a huge alligator skull hanging above the doorway. Big, empty eyesockets seemed to gaze straight through us, and giant, bleached jaws were wide open, as if it was laughing silently.

“Whoa,” I said.

Abe chuckled as he drew up behind us. “Had a b-bit of a run-in with that one.”

“You killed it?” Buck asked.

Abe nodded. “Sure did, just up-river a spell.”

We followed him back out to the porch where he sat down in his rocking chair, pulled out a pipe, and lit it up. The sweet smell of pipe tobacco filled the morning air. Buck and I sat down on the steps and old Abe rocked slowly, puffing on his pipe.

“It was about twenny years ago, when I first got my b-boat there,” he began, nodding down toward the rickety old dock where his boat was tied up. “I set out to head up-river a bit when I got hung up in some reeds. I got out of the boat to p-pull it through when all a sudden it seemed like the whole river just c-come alive all around me! That g-gator was just lyin’ there, like he’d been waitin’ for me the whole time. He must’ve been near twelve feet long! He g-grabbed hold of my leg in a flash to pull me under.”

Abe pulled up the cuff of his trouser and showed us the jagged row of pale scars along his calf.

“If I wouldn’t have had my knife, I’d have been taken down for sure. But before he c-could pull me under, I stuck him through the snout!”

Buck and I listened with our mouths open.

He went on to tell us more stories about gators and such. In fact, he talked for about an hour or so, rocking slowly and smoking his pipe with Mo all drowsy and stretched-out beside him. We listened closely, caught up in his stories and we didn’t even realize how much time had passed. Finally, Abe pulled out a silver watch from his pocket and shook his head.

"You b-boys tryin' to keep me t-talkin' all day," he said, wryly. "It's already close to eleven o'clock, and we ain't even started to look at what needs to g-git done around here."

We got up and Abe showed us a pair of rakes leaning up against the side of the shack. He had us rake the whole area out in front of the cabin which was all a mass of weeds, rocks and pineneedles. We raked and pulled weeds, and after an hour or so, we had cleared most of that away and gotten down to the rich, black earth underneath. All the while, Abe sat up on the porch, whittling away on a chunk of wood, and talking to us about everything from fishing to ancient history and back again.

By the time we had finished, his cabin looked like it had a regular front yard, except without any grass. Buck and I stood back, wiped the sweat from our foreheads and admired our work.

Abe looked it over from his chair. His face was pretty stern, and I couldn't quite tell whether or not he was satisfied with the job we had done. Finally, he nodded. "Not too bad for a c-couple of youngsters."

Buck and I looked at each other. Neither of us was quite sure how to take that.

Then Abe invited us to take a break for lunch so we sat on his porch steps and ate our sandwiches while he rocked and whittled. There was a soft breeze blowing through the forest and the only sounds around us were the rustling of the leaves, and Abe's chair squeaking as he rocked.

I was starting to see how a person could grow to enjoy living out here. The forest was beautiful and things felt so peaceful. Abe's cabin wasn't very big, but it was clean and it seemed comfortable enough.

"Y'know," I said, leaning back, "I never realized how quiet it is out here."

"Yeah," Buck added, chewing on a mouthful of sandwich. "I used to think that a fella'd have to be crazy to want to live out here in the middle of nowhere, but now that I've seen it—it ain't so bad after all."

Abe chuckled. "Well, my place ain't m-much to look at, but the good Lord's always provided for my needs. I g-got a lot to be thankful for."

We were quiet for little while. I started to think about all the folks in town who'd made fun of old Abe or told stories that made him out to be some kind of madman. I remembered having told my share of stories and now I felt a little ashamed. From what I could see, Abe Garner was just an ordinary fellow. And even though folks were treating him unkindly, he didn't seem bitter or angry at all.

Buck had a curious look on his face, like he had been thinking about something important. "You really believe in God and all that?"

Abe raised his eyebrows. "Why sure," he said. "I reckon a body'd have to be mighty foolish not to."

Buck wrinkled up his forehead. "How's that?"

Abe shrugged, and his eyes sparkled a bit. "Well just look around you," he said. "All this *life* didn't just happen by itself. Why everywhere you look, there's miracles happening. Somethin's bein' b-born or hatched every minute. Everything works together so well, and it's all in such a balance, that anyone with half a sense can see it was planned out."

Buck shook his head. "What about all the stuff that *don't* make sense? What about all the folks who're unhappy, or who get treated unfairly? Why don't God plan *those* things out better?"

Abe rubbed his jaw. "Well I s'pose it's all in how you look at it… I s'pose."

Buck grunted. "Looks to me like God don't care a whole lot about some folks."

Abe nodded and puffed on his pipe. "The Lord does p-plenty of things we don't understand directly at first. Sometimes it t-takes a while 'fore we see what he was tryin' to do. If we git too busy b-bein' angry at him, and don't take the time to be quiet and let him do what he wants, we might never see it."

I had been quiet the whole time they were talking. I was lost in my own thoughts and only paid half attention to what they were saying. Finally, I looked up at Abe.

"Why d'you suppose God let my pa get killed?" I asked.

Abe just looked back at me for a few moments, and rubbed his jaw again. The stubble of his half-grown beard made a scratching sound against his hand.

"That's somethin' you may never get a c-clear answer to, Jake," he said, softly. "And I don't reckon there was just one reason for it neither. Some day, maybe years down the road, you might see one or two of the things that's c-come about because of it. Sometimes the Lord uses the deaths of some folks to get the attention of others."

"But why *my* pa? He never did anything wrong. Why not somebody else who deserved to die?"

Abe shrugged. "Seems to me it's the folks that d-deserve to die the most that are the least prepared for it," he said. "Your pa… well, he'd made his peace with God a long time ago. There's a lot of folks what ain't done that yet. Maybe one of the reasons God let your pa die was so that some of them m-might start to think seriously 'bout what's gonna happen to them when they die too."

Buck peeled a chip of paint off the porch step with his thumbnail and snorted. "Still don't make much sense. Seems like God could've used him a lot better alive than dead. He was a lot nicer to me than my own pa is."

"Whutch you mean by that?" Abe asked.

"*My* pa couldn't care less where I am or what I do. He ain't hardly ever home, and when he is, he don't say more'n two words to me. Usually him and Ma just yell at each other."

Abe looked down and his eyes seemed sad again.

"Sometimes I wish *my* pa had gotten killed instead of Jake's," Buck said, sounding disgusted. "Sometimes I *hate* my pa."

Abe stopped rocking and stared down at Buck. He face was stern. "Don't say that."

Buck looked up. "Why not? It's true."

Abe just shook his head like he couldn't believe what he was hearing. "Don't ever say that to his face. Don't ever tell your pa you hate him."

"I don't care! I *do* hate him." Buck's eyes were full of anger, and I had never seen him like that before. He hunched forward on the porch step with his arms wrapped around his knees, not saying a word.

The three of us sat there in silence. Abe's expression softened and he leaned back in his chair.

"It's just that there ain't hardly a man on earth that c-could take hearin' that from one of his own children. N-not that."

Buck shrugged. "My pa don't care," he mumbled under his breath.

We sat in silence for a few more minutes. Abe rocked in his chair and puffed on his pipe. My thoughts went back to my father. There was a part of me that believed what Abe had said, that God probably *did* have his reasons for why he let Pa die.

But still there was a voice inside me saying I'd never make any sense of it. It seemed awfully unfair for Pa to die just so somebody else would believe in God. Buck was right—Pa could've been more useful alive than dead.

Besides, I couldn't think of anyone that knew Pa that would think any differently now that he was dead.

I rubbed my eyes. I was getting so tired of thinking about these things that, deep down, I wished I could've forgotten all about Pa. At that moment, part of me missed him more than ever because I think he would've liked old Abe. But part of me wanted to forget that I had ever known him. It had been only a week since Pa had gotten killed, but somehow it seemed so much longer. It felt like I hadn't seen him for months.

Then Abe got up and went inside. He came back out a minute later with a shotgun.

"Thought we might d-do a bit of hunting."

Mo perked up and wagged his tail. Buck and I jumped up too. I had almost forgotten about our deal, which was the whole reason we had come out to his cabin in the first place.

Abe led us along a trail that followed the river further up into the swamp. The air was humid, and bugs were flying everywhere. I didn't care though, I kept searching along the river bank for any sign of alligators. Abe was busy telling us what kinds of trees we were passing by, and other things about the swamp, but I was only half listening.

We hiked along the path for a while when suddenly Abe paused behind some brush near the river. He pointed out at the water. Several ducks were swimming along the river's edge, just a little further downstream. He leaned over and whispered something to Mo. The old dog tore off and disappeared in the tall weeds. A few seconds later, the ducks took off into the air with a sudden flurry of feathers. Abe raised the gun, aimed, and fired. The sound of the blast echoed through the trees and off into the distance. A second later, one of the ducks dropped into the river like a sack of flour. In a flash, Mo was in the water, paddling out to where the duck had fallen. He scooped it up and swam back to shore with the bird hanging limp in his jaws. He trotted back and dropped it at Abe's feet with no fuss at all.

Abe reached down and scratched Mo behind the ears. "Good boy," he said. "Good dog."

Mo just closed his eyes, and stretched his head forward. I had never seen a dog look as content as Mo did just then.

"Yes sir," Abe said, "don't know what I'd do without ol' Mo. Many a times I'd be out huntin', no thought for where I was or how late it's gettin'. But no matter how lost I mighta been, ol' Mo here could always find the way back."

I was impressed at how good a hunting dog Mo was, but I was still disappointed that I hadn't seen any sign of the big gator. I knew, deep down, it wasn't going to be easy to find. The swamp was a big place, and there were plenty of places for gators to hide out.

At that moment, I felt a sense of hopelessness come over me, and I wondered if I'd ever find that alligator again.

Abe pointed down the river. "Back in there is where the swamp starts gettin' dark and thick. It ain't no p-place to go hikin' or swimmin', so you boys make sure you don't go back in there unless I'm with you, you hear?"

We nodded and peered through the trees to where Abe was pointing. All we could see were mossy tree trunks with thick vines hanging down from their branches. The water was green and dark, and it seemed to have a coat of muck floating on the surface. We couldn't even tell where the shore ended and the river began.

It didn't look very inviting at all.

22

By the time we got back to the cabin, it was already late in the afternoon so we decided to head home before Ma got suspicious. I had hoped I could've gone home and told her that we had found the alligator and killed it. Something inside of me wanted to kill that gator more than anything else in the world. I knew it would never bring Pa back, but I didn't care. It was like all the sorrow of losing him had been rolled up into a big ball of hate that just kept growing inside me. Sometimes, it felt like it was ready to explode. Deep down, I knew it wasn't right to hate something that much but in a way it felt good. And right now it was the only good feeling I had.

I also realized how badly I wanted to prove to everyone that giant gator *was* real and not just part of my imagination. I pictured me and Buck standing on the dock next to the gator's huge carcass while the whole town came out and took pictures and asked questions. But I knew that would have to wait for another day because so far we hadn't seen a thing. I tried not to let my disappointment show. I figured I'd have plenty of chances to find the gator in the days ahead and I didn't want to make a pest out of myself on our first day with old Abe. Otherwise he might've reconsidered our deal and not have taken us with him the next time he went hunting.

When we got home, Buddy was loading a suitcase into the trunk of his car. He told us that he and Aunt Lola were going back to Atlanta in the morning.

"Well Sport," he said, rubbing my hair. "You're the man of the house now. Your ma's gonna need your help more than ever, what with the chores and taking care of Molly and all."

I just nodded and pretended to listen. Buddy didn't seem to know that I already did most of the chores around the house or that aside from washing her own clothes and cooking her own meals, Molly pretty much took care of herself. She seemed to spend most of her time playing with her trucks out in the yard and hardly needed looking-after at all.

Ma had fixed a big supper that night and Buck joined us again for the first time since Pa had died. Aunt Lola cried and wiped her eyes through most of the meal.

"Ann, dear," she said, with her voice all quivering. "Are you *sure* you're going to be okay? Maybe I'd better stay another week—"

"Lola, stop worrying," Ma said, calmly. "We'll be just fine. You and Buddy have already done more than I can ever thank you for."

The rest of the evening went pretty much like that, with Aunt Lola blubbering and Ma consoling her. It almost seemed like it had been Aunt Lola that had lost her husband instead of Ma.

Early that next morning, they said a long and tearful goodbye and drove off. The house seemed so peaceful after they left that I had to admit I wasn't sorry to see them go.

Buck and I went back to Abe's cabin that day and every day that following week. We helped him weed his garden, patch his roof, clean his windows and a hundred other odd jobs around his place. In return, Abe kept up his end of the bargain and took us out hunting with him again. We even took his boat into the swamp a ways to go poking for frogs. We spent quite a bit of time in the swamp that week. Abe taught us about hunting and he even showed us how to whittle. We also learned about some of the best places and times to go fishing and what kind of bait to use and such.

But we never saw any sign of the giant alligator and by the end of the week, I was pretty frustrated. I think Abe knew it too, because of the idea he suggested one day while we were out fishing in his boat.

"A trap?" I said. "What kind of a trap?"

We were drifting slowly along on the river. Abe sat in the bow with a pole in his hand and jiggled his lure a bit as he slowly reeled in his line.

"Well," he said, staring out at the river, "one that'll only spring on somethin' as b-big as a good-sized gator and leave all the smaller animals be."

"How d'you plan to do that?" Buck asked.

"The idea come to me the other d-day," Abe said. "This gator's gotta swim past my place sooner or later. He seems to spend most of his time back in the swamp where it's nice and quiet. And when he gets hungry, he comes back out into the main fork of the river where it's easier to find food."

Abe nodded back in the direction of his cabin. "Now I got some good thick rope back in my shed. We c-could make a sort of net out of it and string it across the river. That gator's got to come by that way eventually."

"And when he does…" I said, getting the drift of Abe's plan.

"We just might tangle him up enough to slow him down a bit," Abe continued. "And I may be able to git a clear shot at him."

"You think that'll really work?" Buck looked skeptical.

Abe shrugged. "I think it's worth a try."

So that afternoon we set about making our trap. We found a spot fifty yards or so downstream from Abe's cabin, where the river narrowed to about thirty feet across and only three or four feet deep. There were plenty of trees along each bank and Abe said that this would be a good place to set our trap.

We took the rope from the tiny shed behind his cabin and cut three sections long enough to reach across the river. We cut the rest of it up into fivefoot lengths. We tied them all together to form a good strong net, with the spaces big enough so that anything smaller than our alligator would be able to swim through without getting caught. Then we tied it off to trees on each side of the river.

Abe rigged the trap so that when the gator tried to swim through, it would pull in just enough slack to get itself good and tangled. We tied a few large rocks along the bottom of the net to weigh down the middle. We also took a big roll of twine, tied one end to the net and ran it back along the path where we tied it off to another tree.

Then we attached some empty tin cans that would clank together and act as a signal when something got caught.

Afterward, we stood back and surveyed our work. The net was pretty well hidden just beneath the surface of the water and all we could see of it were the ends of the rope coming up to the trees on each bank.

"What d'you think?" I asked.

Abe just nodded. "We'll see."

Buck scratched his ear. "I don't think it's gonna work."

Abe and Buck went back to the cabin. I stayed for a while to keep an eye on the trap but nothing happened. I guess I didn't really expect to catch anything right away but still I stood at the edge of the river and peered out into the dark water.

Upstream, the river turned and disappeared around a bend. Downstream, it seemed to widen and lose itself in the dark green backdrop of the swamp. The whole world seem as quiet and as still as death, except for a few birds that called to each other from somewhere in the treetops and the bugs that buzzed past me like cars on a busy highway.

It had been nearly two weeks since Pa had died. Rooster had called off the search for the gator like I knew he would. Everyone seemed sure that the gator Ellis Woods had caught was the one that had killed my father.

Soon folks were back at the park having picnics and such, and even swimming in the river again. Life had gotten back to normal for everyone in Silas.

Everyone but me.

23

That Sunday we went to church. It was the first time we had gone to Sunday service since Pa had died. We sat in the bench where we normally sat except now Pa's space on the aisle was empty. Ma moved over to fill his spot and Molly slid over next to her. But I sat where I normally did, leaving a bigger space between me and Molly.

So there we were, the three of us trying to take up the space of four.

I listened to the sermon that morning. Sam Watson talked about the how we ought to consider the way we treat other folks—especially folks that weren't as well off as we were. He said Jesus had called them 'the least of these' and that whatever we did to them, we did to him as well. I had to admit that was a pretty unsettling thought, especially after having gotten to know Abe. That description seemed to fit him perfectly. So after the morning service, I stopped and asked old Sam about it.

He smiled and said, "Well, sometimes folks get so concerned about themselves they never have time to help out anyone else. Jesus wanted us to be as concerned about other folks as we are about ourselves. Especially folks who're poor and lonely and—"

"Kind of like old Abe Garner," I said, eagerly.

Sam stopped and blinked. And his eyebrows went up a bit. "Well… uh…"

"I mean, he don't seem to have much money," I went on. "And I never seen anybody talk to him much, so he must get lonely too. Don't you think?"

Sam scratched his head and his gaze started darting about the room. "Well yeah, I guess so…"

"So how come nobody ever seems too concerned about him?"

Sam closed his mouth and stayed quiet for a long while. He started to say something a couple times, but he looked as though he couldn't find the right words. Finally, he just sighed and shook his head.

"Because it's a whole lot easier to talk about things than it is to actually do them."

I wasn't sure what he meant by that, but I never got back around to asking him about it. Instead I found myself thinking more and more about the swamp. It seemed like every minute that I wasn't out there, I was wondering if our trap had caught anything yet. It was the first thing I'd ask Abe in the morning when I'd get there, and the last thing I'd check before going home. Nearly another whole week went by and we hadn't caught a thing.

One afternoon we were helping Abe in his garden, when we heard the sound of a motorboat coming down the river. In all the time we had been helping Abe we had never seen another soul come by, so Buck and I dropped our rakes and ran down to the dock to see who it could be. I was afraid that if it was someone heading into the swamp, they might tangle our net and ruin the trap.

We ran out to the dock and peered up river, but we didn't see anyone. The sound of the motor grew steadily louder and finally a boat appeared around the bend, a small fishing boat with one man sitting in the back. He was a round fellow wearing a bright orange life-jacket and fishing hat with mosquito netting over it. As he drew close, he spotted me and Buck and got a curious expression on his face. He looked almost as surprised to see us as we were to see him. He pulled his boat up to the dock and nodded toward us.

"Hello there, boys."

His voice was soft and timid and he looked like he belonged behind a desk in a bank rather than out in the swamp.

We both nodded.

The man looked pretty confused for a moment. He peered around us as if he was looking for some one in particular. Suddenly he smiled and waved.

"Hello, Abe."

We turned around as Abe drew up behind us.

"Hello there Mr. Haley," he said. "How you doin' this afternoon?"

Buck and I looked at each other with our eyebrows raised. How did this fellow know Abe? He was wearing a fancy watch and nice clothes. His skin was pale and he had some kind of cream on his nose to keep the sun from burning it. He seemed totally opposite to Abe in every way.

"Not bad. Not bad… at all," the stranger said, straining as he climbed out of the boat and onto the dock. He stood just a few inches taller than me and looked even rounder up close than he had from a distance. He smiled at me and Buck.

"I see you've got company," he said.

Abe nodded. "This here's Jacob and Buck. They been helpin' me out around the place—you know, gardening and repairs and such."

The man nodded and reached out his hand. "Well that's mighty nice of you boys. My name's Clarence Haley."

We shook his hand, which was soft and doughy and reminded me a little of Buddy's.

"Come on inside." Abe motioned us to follow him up to the cabin.

We went inside and Abe began rummaging through some boxes while Mr. Haley sat down at the table. He took off his hat with the bug netting. He was mostly bald and what hair he did have was all matted down. He untied his bandana and wiped the sweat from his neck and forehead. Then he pulled out a handkerchief to wipe his puffy eyes and then blew his nose in it.

"Them allergies actin' up again?" Abe asked from across the room.

"Well, I got some new medication but it don't seem to help too much." Clarence said. "I just gotta suffer through it, I guess."

Abe came back to the table with a shoe box and sat down. Clarence rubbed his hands together. "What've you got for me today?"

Abe opened the box. Buck and I leaned over his shoulder to peer inside. Abe pulled out a figure of a dog, carved out of wood. It looked just like Mo with sad eyes and floppy ears. Its head was tilted to one side like how a dog looks when its curious about something. I could even see the delicate texture of fur carved into the paws and snout. It was finished with glossy coat of varnish. I had never seen anything like it before.

Clarence whistled. "That's a beauty, Abe."

Buck's jaw hung open and he turned to Abe. "*You* carved that?"

Abe seemed surprised at the question. Then he shrugged and said, "Sure."

Buck just stared at him.

"What else have you got?" Clarence asked.

"Well…" Abe got up and went to the barrels at the back of the room. "I got a few others here."

He brought back an eagle perched on a pedestal with its wings outstretched. It was even more impressive than the dog. I could see the details in every feather. Abe set it down on the table next to the dog. He went back again and returned with an armload of people. He set the figures down carefully. One was a lanky man holding a shovel, and another was a chubby woman with an apron. The last figure was a barefoot boy carrying a fishing pole.

Clarence put on a pair of glasses and inspected the carvings one by one, grunting and nodding to himself. When he was finished, he took off his glasses and wiped his forehead again.

"Some fine work here, Abe. Real fine."

Abe nodded and said, "Thank you kindly. Can I git you some water?"

"Yes please," Clarence said. "Sure is a hot one today."

Abe took an empty pitcher and went outside to the pump. Buck picked up one of the wooden figures and looked it over. "You mean Abe really carved all these?"

"Oh yes," Clarence said. "He's done some of the finest woodwork I've ever seen."

"How long've you known him?" I asked.

"Oooh, about… twenty-five years or so."

"How'd you meet him?"

Clarence thought for a moment. "Well, I guess it's more accurate to say that he met me. See, I own an antique shop up in Chase. I sell all sorts of old furniture and knick-knacks and things. One day this fella walks in with a dusty, old suitcase and shows me some wood carvings he had made. It turns out to be Abe. Well, I had never seen workmanship like that anywhere. He asks if I would mind selling some of his pieces on consignment. I says I'd be happy to—I'm always looking for different things to sell, and at that time my store hadn't been doing all that well financially, if you know what I mean."

Buck and I nodded and listened closely.

Clarence went on. "Well, in only three days I had sold every piece he'd left with me! He comes back the next week with more, so I gladly took them, too. And before I knew it, I had folks comin' by *asking* about those wood carvings, wanting to know if they could get some too. So I worked out a deal with Abe to buy his pieces outright so he wouldn't have to keep comin' all the way up to Chase to collect his money. I told him I'd come by his place to pick them up once a month. I come to find he makes these all himself out here in this old shack. I started selling so many, old Abe couldn't hardly keep up with the demand. Pretty soon I got folks making special requests for things. I'd tell Abe what they wanted and he'd carve it! These days I got folks from three counties coming all the way to my store just to buy one of those wood carvings I ain't never seen anything like it, no sir."

Then he chuckled and shook his head. "And old Abe knows what he's worth too. He knows what folks'll pay for his work, but he always quotes me a fair price. I used to try hagglin' with him, but he don't budge a bit. In twenty-five years he's never settled for a dollar less than what he thinks they're worth. But he's never asked for a penny more."

At that point, Abe came back with the water. He and Clarence chatted for a while about the weather and other small talk. They laughed and talked like old friends. After a half hour or so, Clarence carefully packed the carvings into a bag that he had brought with him and handed Abe a thick envelope. Then he got into his boat and started back up the river.

"Nice to meet you boys," he said, waving back to us. "See you next month, Abe."

After he had disappeared around the bend, Buck and I turned to Abe.

"How come you never told us you could carve like that?" Buck demanded.

Abe blinked, looking genuinely surprised, and shrugged. "You never asked."

Then he brought us inside and opened the chest at the foot of his bed. Inside were several more pieces that he was still working on. Some were figures of animals, some were of people. There was even a small box that contained several pieces of a chess set that he had been making. The detail and craftsmanship were amazing. He showed us the knives, chisels and other tools that he used. I suddenly felt ashamed as Abe's comment sunk in.

You never asked.

Abe was right. I hadn't really shown any interest in him, other than in how he could help me kill that alligator. I knew he could whittle—he even tried to show us how—but I had never paid any attention to what he was making. I had noticed the figures on the barrels in his cabin, but I had never looked close enough at them to see their real beauty. They had been sitting there the whole time, but I never bothered to really *look* at them. I had been so concerned with what he could do for me, I never stopped long enough to appreciate anything else about him. I grew a little sad as I realized how selfish I had been.

Suddenly, a loud clatter outside brought me up from my thoughts and we all rushed out to the porch to see what was happening. It was the signal for our trap!

The tin cans were clanking together so furiously and the twine was shaking so hard, that for a second I thought someone had been hiding in the woods and was just yanking on the string to play a prank on us. A rush of excitement swelled up inside me like a tidal wave as I realized that it wasn't a prank at all.

Something was caught in the net!

24

Buck and I took off down the path. Behind us, we heard Mo barking and Abe calling after us.

"Buck! Jacob! Don't touch anything!"

We got to the bank where the trap was set and stopped dead in our tracks. Out in the middle of the river the water was churning and frothing. It looked like an underground volcano had erupted causing the whole river to come to a boil. The ropes of the net shook and twisted so violently, I was sure they were going to snap. I stood on the bank, peering into the river but I couldn't see anything under the murky water.

Suddenly, an enormous shape curled up out of the water—a huge black tail with leathery ridges along the back! It looked as thick as a tree trunk, and as it slapped back down again, it sprayed water clear across the river. A chilling memory flashed back into my head. I had seen it before…

The tail whipped upward a second time and splashed down.

And then we saw it.

Great black jaws rose up out of the foam, apread open so wide they looked like they could've swallowed me whole. A pink tongue, like a thick slab of ham, curled back behind a row of yellow teeth. The beast made a hissing growl so deep, my ribs vibrated. It was like some dragon rising up from the swamp. It lifted its whole body almost entirely out of the water, revealing its thick, black hide. Water streamed off its sides and between the two rows of ridges that ran along its back. For an instant, I could see the ropes wrapped tightly around its neck and legs but they looked no bigger than ordinary twine compared to the alligator's great size. It twisted its massive bulk around, exposing its pale underbelly. Then its whole body crashed back down again, soaking us with a spray of murky water.

Buck just stood there with his mouth open. His eyes were wide and his face had gone all white.

"It's… it's… *huge*!" he whispered.

Then I heard a loud snap as one of the ropes beside me broke. The gator rolled and spun under the surface. A second later, both ropes on the far side of the river snapped as well. They slipped into the water and disappeared.

It was getting away!

I spotted the last rope, looped around the base of the tree beside me. It was frayed, and looked like it could break any moment. I dove into the mud and grabbed for it.

"*Help me*!" I cried to Buck, but he just stood there, staring at the gator like he was in a trance.

I tried to pull the gator closer to shore, but it didn't budge. I might as well have been trying to pull a tree out by its roots. But I couldn't let go. I had to keep it from getting away.

Then I heard Abe shout, "Don't touch that!"

I turned and saw Abe hurrying down the path, carrying his shotgun. Mo bounded toward us, howling excitedly. Just then, the rope went loose in my grasp and I looked up to see that the gator had rolled toward me, creating slack, but in a flash it spun back the other way, tearing the rope from my hands. It snapped from the tree like a piece of thread and slipped into the water.

Abe reached the bank, raised his shotgun and fired. The sound of the blast echoed in the distance, but it was too late. I could see the gator's ridged back racing off down the river with the ropes trailing behind it. In a few moments, it had disappeared into the murky waters of the swamp.

I sat in the mud, staring down the river. I couldn't believe what I had just seen. That was it! That was the alligator we were after. And we had almost killed it! Now I knew I hadn't imagined it. Now I knew what had killed my father. If I *had* any doubts before, they were gone now.

But so was the gator.

I knelt in the mud, heart pounding, trying to catch my breath. We had come so close. If the ropes would have held for just a few more seconds, then maybe Abe would've had a shot.

Just a few more seconds…

I felt a hand on my shoulder. Abe stood over me. "You okay?" he asked, softly.

For a moment, I couldn't answer. Disappointment hit me like a wave, knocking the wind out of me. I felt like I'd been kicked in the stomach.

"Are you hurt?" Abe said.

I knew I wasn't injured. At least not physically. I shook my head. "I'm okay.

He helped me up and I noticed that Buck was still staring out at the water where the gator had been. The surface had settled and was now nearly calm again. It almost seemed like the alligator had never even been there, like the struggle we had just seen had never happened.

Buck shook his head. "I don't believe it."

Abe peered down the river, toward the swamp. "That was him alright. Sure enough."

Buck turned to Abe. "I ain't never seen an alligator that *big*! I don't believe it."

I wiped the mud off my hands and jeans. "Believe it," I said. "*That's* what killed my pa."

"Ain't like no gator I ever seen," Abe said.

We headed back toward the cabin. Buck kept shaking his head and saying how he couldn't believe what he'd just seen. I had to admit that I was in shock myself. The gator was even bigger than I remembered.

We got back to the cabin and sat down on the porch. My disappointment now felt like an icy river. Our trap had failed and there wasn't enough rope left to make another one. Besides, it could be weeks before the gator came back that way again.

I shook my head. I couldn't let myself give up that easily! We had come so close to killing it, we couldn't quit now. At least we knew it was still in the area, somewhere deep in the swamp. But the it was a big and dangerous place. I had heard stories of folks who had gotten lost or drowned in a bog and were never seen nor heard from again. I knew better than to go back in there myself.

Then I remembered something Abe had told us. "You said you had seen it once while you were out in the swamp," I said.

Abe nodded. "Yep, way back by the old boat house."

"You think that's where it might be headed?"

Abe rubbed his jaw. "It's possible—but don't get no ideas. That ain't no place to go huntin' gators."

"But *you* know your way around there," I said. "Can't we just go back and take a look?"

Abe shook his head. "Too dangerous. You seen the size of that beast. He could tip my boat with one slice of that tail."

"But we might never find it again," I pleaded. "This could be our only chance."

"Patience, Jake," Abe said. "The one thing you need to learn about huntin' or anything is patience. Some things take time. You can't just go rushin' in after that thing."

"But I've *been* patient," I said. "We've kept up our side of the bargain. We've helped you around here. Just take us back there once. Just once?"

Abe gave a deep sigh. He got up from his rocking chair, walked to the edge of the porch and stared out into space. After several seconds he turned around and his eyes looked kind of sad.

"Alright," he said. "But not today."

As we rode home that afternoon, I was so excited I could hardly contain myself. Even Buck was eager to get started. Now that he had seen the gator himself, he seemed to have a whole new outlook on our mission.

"I gotta admit," he said as we rode into town. "I didn't really believe you at first—about how big this thing is."

I shrugged. "That's okay, nobody did."

"That's gotta be the biggest alligator anywhere in these parts—probably in the whole world! Maybe we'll even get our pictures in the paper."

"Well, we gotta find it first," I said. "And that ain't gonna be easy."

But I didn't care how difficult it would be. Somehow I knew we would find it. Then I could prove to everyone that I had been right all along. Even though our trap had failed, I knew that gator was still around and I couldn't wait to get started. We weren't going to just sit around any longer for that gator to come to us. Now *we* were going to find *it*!

25

We were so excited that we decided to stop at Buckman's Drugstore for sodas. It was almost four o'clock and, as usual, Yancey, Mort, Jolly and Clem were all there.

"Well just look at you," Yancey said, shaking his head at me as we walked in. "From the looks of it, you'd think dirty clothes were in style these days."

Mort and Jolly glanced up from their chess game and chuckled. "What happened to you?" Mort asked, looking over his glasses at me.

I wanted to tell them what had happened but I figured I'd better not. "We were just out fishin' is all," I said, casually.

"Shoot," Jolly laughed. "Looks like you boys spent more time diggin' for worms than actually doin' any fishing."

Yancey looked at me suspiciously. "Come on," he said, with a wry grin. "There's more to it than that. What happened?"

I shrugged and looked down. "Nothing," I said, but I couldn't stop grinning.

Yancey chuckled. "Come on now, tell us what *really* happened."

I could hear Buck on the stool beside me, trying to stifle his laughter. I knew either we had to leave or else I'd end up telling them everything. But I couldn't hold it in any longer.

"We saw the alligator!" I blurted out.

Yancey looked at me with his grin still on his face. After a few moments, it melted away. He tilted his head, as if he was thinking maybe he had misunderstood what I had said.

"How's that?"

"The one that killed my Pa," I said slowly, so he would understand. "We saw it today."

Yancey continued to stare at me. His grin was gone now and I couldn't figure out what kind of expression it had changed to. He almost looked like he was a little sad, like he felt sorry for me for some reason. By now I was getting confused. I looked over to Mort and Jolly, but they weren't smiling either. I couldn't figure out why they were reacting that way. Had they misunderstood me? Didn't they hear what I had said?

"What's the matter?" I asked.

Yancey started to say something but then he paused for a moment and glanced around the room.

"Well… ummm… where did you see it?"

"Out near the swamp," I said. I glanced at Buck and he gave me a look like he thought I had made a mistake by telling them the truth. I was beginning to think so, too.

"I see," Yancey said. "So… you've been out there, have you? Out in the swamp?"

"No," I said. "No, we weren't actually *in* the swamp. Just up-river a ways from it—"

"That ain't no place for you boys to be playin' around," Mort said, gruffly.

"We weren't playin' around," Buck snapped. "We were just helpin' out old man Garner—"

I cringed. *Oh no. Don't tell them about—*

"*Abe Garner*?" Clem said, turning from the doorway. He looked as if he didn't know whether to be angry or surprised. "You boys ain't been hangin' around *his* place have you?"

By now, everyone—including Yancey—had a look of shock on their faces. My mind was spinning. How would we ever get out of this one? I shot Buck an angry glance and he looked down at his feet like he knew he'd made a big mistake. The situation was going from bad to worse and I had to figure out how to head it off before we got ourselves into even bigger trouble. Unfortunately, my mouth started to move before I knew what to say.

"He ain't like everyone says," I heard myself saying. "I don't know why nobody likes him. He never did anything wrong! You never even took the time to get to know him. All you can do is make up stories and poke fun at him—but he never did anything to you!"

I could see Clem Anderson's temper coming to a boil. His eyes began to bulge at the same time his tiny mouth puckered up even tighter and the gnarled veins on his neck and scalp began to pop out. He pointed his walking-stick at us and shook it.

"Don't *you*..." he hissed. "Don't you tell *me* about Abe Garner! I've known Abe Garner since before your pa was even born!"

"Clem," Mort said, sternly. But Clem just ignored him.

"How dare you tell me *I'm* makin' up stories—"

"Clem!"

"—when you don't even know the truth, you... you little... *brats*!"

"*Clem*!" Mort slapped his hand down on the table, sending several of his wooden chess pieces bouncing to the floor.

Buck and I sat there in shock. I had never seen Clem Anderson get so mad about anything before in my life. He slowly regained his composure, took out a handkerchief from his trouser pocket and wiped his forehead. His hands trembled. He looked around at the others who all seemed surprised by his outburst as well, and then down at his feet like he was embarrassed. After a long awkward silence, he mumbled something under his breath and walked out.

The screen door slammed shut and the rest of us just sat there in silence.

After a few moments, Yancey sighed and rubbed his temples. "Jake, it ain't as though we don't like old Abe," he said. "It's just that we don't think it's a very good idea for you two to be spending so much time out there. Mort's right, that swamp's a dangerous place."

"But I *had* to go," I said. "Everyone thinks Ellis Woods caught the gator that killed my pa, but they're wrong. It's still out there. It's still alive!"

Yancey put his hand on my shoulder. "Jake, I know how much you want to—"

"But I *saw* it," I said. "We *both* did."

"Now Jake," Mort said, sternly. "There's plenty of gators out in that swamp. *Plenty* of 'em. Big ones too. Now you're just gonna get yourself hurt if you keep goin' back out there on some wild goose chase. We've seen too many kids get hurt foolin' around out there over the years."

I started to say something but then stopped. I knew it would be no use. I wasn't going to convince them. I don't even know why I bothered to try. No one would believe me until they could see it for themselves. I got up to leave.

"This ain't no ordinary alligator," I said. "But you'll see. I'm gonna kill it. Then you'll see!"

With that, Buck and I left. As we rounded the corner of the building where we had parked our bikes, we found Clem Anderson standing there, tall and gaunt, with a grim look on his face. He didn't seem angry any longer. In fact, he looked a little sad.

"You kids don't even know the half of it," he said, shaking his head. His eyes had a faraway look in them. "Folks 'round here always want to sweep things under the rug—want to pretend it never happened."

"What're you talking about?" Buck asked.

Clem gave us a stern look. "Abe Garner," he said. "You want to know why he lives all alone out in that swamp?"

Then I remembered the time Clem said Yancey didn't know the real reason Abe was living out there all by himself. At the time, it made me very curious. I guess I had forgotten all about it until now. Now, I wasn't too sure that I wanted to know.

"He's a murderer is why!" Clem's face twisted into a look of disgust. "Killed his own wife!"

Buck and I looked at each other in disbelief. I didn't know what to say. I wasn't even sure how to feel. Abe had never said anything about even *having* a wife. I thought about all the time we had spent with him over the last two weeks. Sure, maybe two weeks wasn't a very long time to get to know someone but Abe hardly seemed like a murderer to me.

"I don't believe you," I said.

Clem chuckled coldly and leaned close. "Don't believe me? Take a ride over to the library in Comstock and look it up in the papers. Thirty-two years ago last April. Killed her in front of his own son. Burned down his own house in a drunken rage. Police never found enough evidence to convict him but I know he done it. Everybody knows he done it."

I had heard stories about Abe being a murderer before but nothing like this. I looked at Buck again and he seemed a little unsure. I didn't know what to say. Clem Anderson wasn't known to be the most reliable person in Silas. But still…

"We gotta go," I said, climbing on my bike.

We headed off for home, but I could hear Clem chuckling as we rode away.

"Go see for yourselves if you don't believe me," he laughed. "Go and see for yourselves."

26

Lightning skipped across the clouds in jagged streaks that lit up the darkness. Rain whipped at the windows and booming cracks of thunder shook the whole house. The wind moaned like a restless spirit, bending the trees under its force.

It was almost midnight when Buck and I spread out our sleeping bags on the floor of my room to watch the storm. Buck's father was home for a couple of days, so Buck had come over to spend the night and get away from all the bickering.

Neither of us seemed to be in the mood to talk much that night. But we couldn't fall asleep either.

Clem Anderson's words kept nagging at me, and doubts circled inside my head like vultures. There was no good reason to believe what he had said about Abe. But still, I couldn't help feeling a little afraid. What if Abe really was a murderer? Why didn't he ever say anything about having a wife? How could we trust going out into the swamp alone with him? It seemed like all my hopes for finding that gator were sinking again.

Buck turned to me and asked, "D'you think it's true?"

I shrugged. "About Abe? I don't know."

"What if he really *did* kill his wife?"

"We don't know that for sure," I said. "Clem Anderson doesn't know everything."

A flash of lightning streaked across the sky.

"Well, I don't like the idea of goin' back into the swamp with him," Buck said. "That kind of gives me the creeps."

A loud clap of thunder rattled the house.

I sat up. "If Abe Garner had wanted to kill us, he would've done it by now. He just don't seem like a murderer to me."

"Yeah, but what if he's just pretending to be nice," Buck said. "What if he's just doin' that to fool us. Or what if he has episodes—y'know, like sometimes he just goes crazy and kills people. Maybe we just ain't seen that side of him yet."

Another flash of lightning lit up the room.

"*Episodes*?" I laughed, uneasily. "Where'd you hear that?"

Another crash of thunder shook our ribs.

"Don't laugh," Buck said. "I read it somewhere. A guy can be perfectly normal one minute and then all of a sudden—*wham!* He just goes crazy. Something happens to trigger it, like a loud noise, or somebody mentions a word or something. It happens all the time. I read it"

"Then let's go up to Comstock to see if we can find out what really happened," I said. "Abe is the only one who can help us find that alligator and I ain't about to let myself get scared off by Clem Anderson."

Outside the storm continued to rage.

The next morning we decided to get an early start. Comstock was a good five miles from Silas and the library was only open until noon on Saturdays.

Now the public library in Comstock is one of the oldest buildings in the whole county. It sits right in the center of town, across the street from a park where they've got a big statue of Seth Meade between two cannons from the Civil War. Seth Meade had done something famous during the war, although no one could remember exactly what it was. In any case, his grandson Cyrus paid a lot of money to have this bronze statue made of him so I guess most folks figured it must've been pretty important.

I had only been to the library there once or twice before. It was a big place with stone walls that were packed with shelves and shelves of books. We went to the main desk and asked the librarian if we could see where they kept all the old newspapers. She looked suspicious at first, so I told her I was trying to find an old newspaper article about my grandfather. She led us to a big musty room with even more shelves inside it. On the shelves were stacks of large cardboard boxes that were labeled by year. I told her what month and year I was looking for and she led us to a spot near the back of the room.

"They're organized by month," she said, pointing to a box marked *April*. "Now be careful how you handle these—they're *very* old. And let me know when you're finished."

She left us alone in the room. A nervous feeling came over me as I opened the box. I wasn't sure I wanted to find out what had really happened. The box smelled like a musty attic. I pulled out the first issue and examined the headlines. It read *Chase Clarion* across the top and each issue was mounted in a sort of photo album to preserve it. The plastic-covered pages were yellow and a little faded but still readable.

I flipped through that first issue but didn't see any articles about Abe. Buck took another one out as well and flipped through it. It felt strange to see those old newspapers, almost like we had gone back in time. There were stories and photos of people we didn't know, most of whom had probably died long ago.

We had looked through about ten or twelve issues when Buck suddenly stopped. "I think I found it."

He pointed to a photograph on the front page. The picture was of a black man standing in front of what looked like the charred remains of a house. He seemed to be staring at the camera with dull, empty eyes. It looked like it might've been Abe but I couldn't tell for sure. I could make out the shadowy figure of a small boy in the background huddled on what had been the front porch of the house, clutching some kind of stuffed animal. Above the picture the headline read: *Taylor's Bend Man Suspected in Wife's Death.*

I scanned the short article. "Yeah, it's him alright. It says, 'Sheriff's deputies questioned Abraham Garner regarding the sudden death of his wife Margaret yesterday afternoon. Bruises on the victim's body led deputies to suspect a history of beatings at the hands of her husband. Garner is also suspected of being responsible for the fire which burned down his home in Taylor's Bend three days ago. Authorities determined that the fire was due to negligence on the part of Garner who had been improperly storing gasoline in his garage. Sheriff Burdick says at this time no formal charges in Mrs. Garner's death have been filed but the investigation is still ongoing.'"

"What else does it say?" Buck asked.

I shrugged. "That's all. Let's check some more papers and see if there's any other articles about him."

We spent the next hour or so looking through the rest of the April box as well as May and June, but we didn't see anything else written about Abe. It was as if the newspaper had just forgotten all about him.

"It don't sound too good," Buck said. "Sounds like he beat his wife to death."

I shook my head. "There's got to be more to it than that. How come they never wrote anything else about him? How come they never arrested him?"

Buck shrugged and we sat quietly for a few moments.

"Well then, let's ask *him*," I said, at last.

Buck stared at me and blinked. "Ask *Abe?* Are you crazy? What if that triggers another episode?"

"It ain't gonna trigger no episode," I said. "And we gotta find out what really happened."

27

It was almost noon when we left the library. We started back toward Silas, still arguing about whether or not talking to Abe about his wife's death was a good idea. I had to admit, I was a little nervous myself. There was no way to be sure that Abe would tell the truth, but I had also learned not to put too much trust in newspapers either. Pa had often said "Never believe everything you read except what you read in the Bible."

So that afternoon, we rode out to Abe's cabin. He was sitting on his porch, whittling, with Mo sleeping beside him. He puffed on his pipe and nodded to us as we came up.

"Afternoon boys," he said. "Thought for a while, you might not be comin' by today."

I kicked at the dirt. "Yeah, well… we had some things to do, so…"

Abe started to chuckle. "What's wrong? You look like you got somethin' on your mind."

I glanced at Buck. "Well, no. Not really."

Abe stopped whittling and stared at us. "What's the matter?"

I couldn't think of how to start or what to say. I didn't want to tell him what Clem Anderson had said. I didn't want him to know the kinds of things folks were saying about him back in town. I also didn't want it to look like we didn't trust him or that we had been snooping around. Suddenly, I had an idea.

"Well, me and Buck were talking last night," I said. "And we were just wondering what made you decide to come live way out here in the swamp all by yourself."

Abe narrowed his eyes for a moment. Then he shook his head. "That's a long, sad story. I don't like to burden other folks with it."

"It ain't no burden," I said, looking over at Buck. "We'd really like to know."

Abe nodded and sighed. "Well, I used to live up in Taylor's Bend—just outside Chase. That's been more'n thirty years ago now. Back then I used to work for Cyrus Meade, driving truck and makin' deliveries and such. The pay wasn't much, but I had a plan. I was married at the time you see, and my wife, Maggie… well, she was doin' housekeepin' for the Meades and a few other of the wealthier folks around Chase."

Abe looked down and started whittling again. "Well, after a few years, we had managed to scrape together enough savings for me to buy a truck of my own. It was an old broke-down pickup, but I had learned a few things workin' for Cyrus and so I managed to get it runnin' again. Pretty soon, I had gotten some odd jobs on the weekends, haulin' old junk away for folks. So I started to earn some extra money. Before I knew it, I was makin' as much on the weekend as I did workin' for Cyrus during the week."

Buck and I sat down on the porch steps and listened closely.

Abe went on. "After a few more years, we had saved enough money to buy a newer truck, so I quit workin' for Cyrus altogether and started workin' for myself. We kept saving our money and soon Maggie and I were able to buy a little place of our own. It was right about then we had our son, Paul. Maggie was able to quit her housekeeping jobs 'cause I had more'n enough work to keep me busy."

"So what happened?" Buck asked.

Abe chuckled a bit, but there was a sad look in his eyes. I had seen it before in Yancey Buckman. And also in Pa.

Abe shrugged. "Made the mistake of hirin' a white fella to work for me. He was a good man—hard worker'n all, but some folks just couldn't abide seein' a white man workin' for no colored folk."

"What'd they do?" I asked.

Abe shrugged. "Made it clear I wasn't welcome no more. Ran me off my own land."

He sighed and drew in deep on his pipe. He sat there rocking and staring off into space. I had never heard any of this before. None of the stories about Abe had ever mentioned anything about him having a wife or working for Cyrus Meade, or anything like that at all.

Now, I had never met Cyrus Meade before, but everyone in town knew who he was. He owned half the land in Chase county it seemed, and he and his wife, Virginia, still lived in their big mansion north of Chase. Every once in a while, the newspaper would have an article about some big donation that they had made to one charity or other. Of course, Cyrus owned the Chase newspaper as well.

Now it was time for the tough question. I swallowed hard. "So whatever happened to your wife?"

A smile came across Abe's face as he stared out at the river. "Maggie was a good woman," he said. "She never complained at all, and she always stuck by me."

Then his smile faded a bit. "She passed away 'bout that same time. She had a weak heart and I don't think it was able to take losin' everything we had worked for all those years."

"So who was it that had run you off your land like that?" Buck asked.

Abe shook his head. "Can't rightly say. I never got a good look at any of 'em. They beat us both up pretty bad, right in front of our own child. And they threatened to beat him too. They burned down our house and the garage where I kept my truck. We lost everything that we had worked for all those years."

"Why didn't you call the sheriff?" Buck asked.

Abe shrugged. "Well, we did. But back then there wasn't no law against runnin' colored folk off their own land. No law what got enforced at least."

"So you came out here to hide out?" I said.

Abe shook his head. "Naw, I stayed in Taylor's Bend for a few years, working odd jobs, tryin' to raise my son, but no one wanted to keep me on very long. Rumors had spread about me gettin' drunk and burnin' down my house. Some folks even said I had killed my own..."

His voice cracked and he looked down at the piece of wood he had been carving. He was quiet for a long while. I couldn't think of anything to say.

Finally, Abe looked up again. "Anyways, by then my son Paul was gettin' older. He started to get in fights with other kids because of all the things they'd be sayin 'bout me. He'd even get mad at me 'cause I wasn't doin' anything about it. He thought I was wrong not to fight back. I told him 'bout how the Lord had said to turn the other cheek. But Paul wouldn't listen. He was goin' around with the wrong kind of friends, and they told him he needed to fight back. They said that's what it would take to get justice. So they taught him how to fight. And they taught him it was okay to hate the folks who hated him.

"Then one day when he was about fifteen, we got in an argument over what he was doin'. He called me a coward. Said he hated me and even blamed his Ma's death on me. He ran out that night. Packed up all his things and ran away. That was twenty-five years ago and I ain't seen him since."

Abe paused and whittled for a few more minutes. Buck and I watched quietly. His fingers handled the knife with such ease and confidence, it seemed like it was just an extension of his hand. Several other knives and chisels were tucked inside the front pocket of his overalls. I hadn't noticed them before, but every so often he would reach up and pluck one out to use for a few moments, and then slip it back into his pocket. He performed the move so smoothly, I hadn't even been aware he was doing it. It seemed as though I was watching him work for the very first time. I was amazed at the speed and steadiness of his hands. It was as if there was already a finished piece of work hidden inside the wood and Abe was just cutting away all the excess pieces to uncover it.

After a while Abe continued talking. "Not long after that, I came out here to the swamp. I couldn't get anyone to hire me on for very long, so I had to try to earn a living some other way. I had always fancied myself a pretty fair hand at woodcarving. I made a few pieces and brought 'em up to Chase to see if Mr. Haley would sell 'em at his store. He agreed to it on the condition that he wouldn't tell folks that I had made them. He figured it would be safer that way, and that was alright by me. I've been out here ever since. I earn enough money to git by and I got a lot to be thankful for."

Buck shook his head. "After all the things folks done to you, how can you say you're still thankful?"

Abe paused for a moment, staring at the half-carved figure in his hands. Then he shrugged. "Because I know the Lord has a purpose for everything he allows us to suffer through. I guess we're a little like wood in a way. God wants to make something special of us. And even though the whittlin' may be painful at times, he never makes a mistake."

He continued carving. Tiny chips peeled off and dropped to the floor like leaves from a tree. With every sliver Abe carved off, the wood took on a new shape. And with each piece he cut away, it was becoming more than it had been before.

"How come you never told us any of this before?" I asked after a moment.

Abe just shrugged and smiled. "You never asked."

I just shook my head. So that was Abe's story. He had been mistreated most of his life, but he didn't sound bitter or angry. I wondered how a man could lose so much and still have the kind of peace Abe seemed to have. I wondered how many others really knew the truth about old Abe. People had spent so much time embellishing old stories and making up new ones that no one even considered finding out what had really happened. And I had been as guilty as everyone else.

We all sat quietly for several minutes. A light breeze blew through the forest and the leaves rustled gently. Suddenly, Mo perked up his ears and growled. Underneath the sound of the wind was something else. It began as a soft rumble, distant and low, and slowly grew louder.

"What is it?" I asked.

Abe got up and walked to the edge of the porch. He peered through the trees back down the old dirt path that led to his cabin. The rumble grew steadily louder. He turned back to us and his face was serious.

"Someone's coming."

28

The rumbling grew steadily louder. We stood on the porch steps and peered down the path where I could see a dark shape moving among the trees. After a few minutes the sheriff's truck emerged into the clearing.

"The sheriff?" I said. "What's *he* doin' here?"

But the figure that stepped out of the truck wasn't the sheriff at all. It was his deputy, Billy Ray Martin. He was in full uniform with the brim of his hat pulled down just above his mirrored sunglasses. He stood there with his hands on his hips, tapping his fingers lightly against his holster and chewing heavily on a mouthful of gum.

A tall, husky man wearing jeans and a t-shirt got out the other side of the truck. Buck gasped. "Pa."

Earl Miller sucked the last bit of smoke from his cigarette and flicked the butt off into the dirt. He held his breath for a moment before letting the smoke out, first through his nose, then through his mouth.

They walked up to the porch. Billy Ray looked around and scratched the back of his neck.

"You boys okay?"

Buck and I shrugged. "Yeah."

Billy Ray nodded, still looking around. "You mind tellin' me what you're doin' out here?"

"Just doin' some fishing," I said.

"Uh-huh," said Billy Ray. He chewed his gum even louder and looked back at our bikes that were leaning up against a tree. "Where's your fishing poles?"

Then I remembered that we had come straight from the library in Comstock. We hadn't brought our poles with us today.

"Uuhh," I stammered, trying to think of an excuse.

Billy Ray didn't wait for one. "We hear you boys been spendin' quite a bit of time out here lately."

At that point Abe spoke up. "The b-boys been k-kind enough to hep me out r-r-round the place a bit," he said. "You know, p-patchin' the roof and w-weedin' the garden. And in exchange, I been t-takin' 'em out to do some f-fishin' every once in a while. B-but they just stopped by for a visit today… j-just a visit."

Earl Miller grunted and shook his head.

"Well now..." Billy Ray looked at me and Buck, ignoring Abe all together. "You boys ever think to let your folks know where you was goin'?"

I looked down. "I told my ma we were fishing."

"Did you tell her where?"

I shrugged and kicked at the dirt. There was a long silence. All I could hear was Billy Ray chewing and popping his gum.

Finally he said, "Your ma's been mighty worried about you, Jake."

I shrugged again. "We always go fishin'. She knows that."

"And how about you, Buck?" Billy Ray said sternly, turning to Buck. "Your pa wakes up this morning only to find your bed ain't even been slept in. We spent the better part of the day out lookin' for you boys. There's a lot of folks back in town who're pretty upset. That was mighty irresponsible of you two."

"Sorry," we both mumbled.

"Then we hear tell you been spendin' all your time out here in the swamp, huntin' alligators," Billy Ray went on. "Now, you know better'n that. This ain't no place for you kids to be playin' around."

I could feel my anger growing, like a kettle coming to a boil. We were getting so close to finding the alligator and now Billy Ray was going to ruin everything. We never should have stopped by the drugstore. We never should've told those old men what we had been up to. I was tired of everyone telling me how dangerous it was out here in the swamp. I was tired of being told where I could spend my time. And I was sick and tired of being talked down to by adults.

"What do you care?" I muttered.

Billy Ray stopped chewing his gum and his eyebrow went up. "What did you say?"

I swallowed my fear, gathered my courage and looked him in the eye as best I could. "I mean… there ain't no law against fishin' out here."

Billy Ray leaned close. I could see my reflection in his sunglasses and smell the scent of cigarettes and bubblegum on his hot breath. He stared at me for a long while. His face was stern and cold. "Don't *ever* talk back to me again," he growled. "You understand?"

For a moment I thought he was going to hit me. His gaze bored right through me from behind his sunglasses and I felt a wave of tingling, hot pricks all over my skin. Sweat started to bead on my forehead.

I looked down and nodded. "Yes, sir."

After a few more seconds he straightened up. "Good. Now let's get your bikes in the truck. We're takin' you boys home."

I looked up. "How come?"

Billy Ray turned around and headed back to the truck. "Because your ma sent us to fetch you is why. She don't want you coming out here no more."

Earl Miller grunted. "You too, Buck."

Buck was silent. He hung his head down and followed his father back to the truck. I turned to Abe as a feeling of helplessness started to grow inside me. I guess I had hoped he would've said something to defend himself. And us.

"Do something," I pleaded in a whisper.

But he just stood there with a sad look in his eyes and shook his head. "You best go now, Jake."

I couldn't believe what I was hearing. He of all people should've known that I couldn't give up now. I wouldn't give up. He had seen the alligator himself. He was the only one who believed me. He was the only one who really knew.

But all he did was shake his head. "It'd probably be best if you didn't come back no more."

"*What*?" I gasped. "But we had a deal."

"Goin' after that alligator," Abe said, "it ain't a good idea. The deputy's right."

"But we know right where it's at," I argued. "We can't give up now!"

"It's too dangerous, Jake."

"But we're so *close*!"

Abe put his hand on my shoulder. "You gotta think of your ma now." His voice was soft and grim. "She needs you at home. Don't worry about that gator, I'll find it eventually."

"No!"

"Remember what I said about being patient? It'll come by here again sooner or later and I'll kill it for you. Don't worry."

I felt like I was in a daze. I couldn't believe I had come so close and now it was all being torn away from me. I knew I couldn't trust some one else to kill that alligator—not even Abe. Ellis Woods had said he was going to kill it but he had gotten the wrong one. I couldn't trust anyone else again, not ever.

Billy Ray and Earl started to load our bikes into the back of the pickup. I glanced at them and then back at Abe.

"But we're so close," I said again, trying to keep my voice low. "We had a *deal!*"

Abe stared down at me. Suddenly, his eyes looked kind of peaceful and I couldn't figure out why.

"Let it go, Jake," he said. "Killin' that thing ain't gonna bring your pa back. And it ain't gonna ease your pain neither. You got to think about your ma now. That gator took you pa from her and now its takin' you away too, a little bit at a time."

"That's why I got to *kill* it!" I said, clenching my fists. That alligator had ruined my whole family. We had been torn apart and ruined forever, all because of that stupid animal. It had no sense or purpose. It couldn't reason or be reasoned with. I *had* to kill it—it deserved to die! And Abe Garner had been my last hope. I couldn't believe he was going to give up now. Not now!

But he just shook his head. "You can't hate that thing, Jake," he said. "Don't let yourself hate like that."

He walked past me a few feet and watched as Earl and Billy Ray finished loading up the bikes. Then he turned around, shaking his head. "Hate like that… it's like a leather boot. Brand new, it's all stiff and awkward. But if you wear it long enough, eventually it gets broke in. Pretty soon it gets comfortable and you don't *want* to take it off. And before you know it, you forget how. Next thing you know you *can't* take it off no more 'cause it's become a part *of* you. Like a second skin. And you can't remember feelin' any other way."

He rested his big hand on my shoulder and frowned.

"And you're too young to hate like that, Jake," he said. "Don't hate like that."

For a moment—for a brief moment—my anger softened. I felt like there was a part of me deep inside that knew what Abe had said was true. And just for a moment, my fists opened and my gaze fell.

Then Billy Ray started up the truck and yelled out the window, "Let's go, Jake!"

And that was when the other part of me—the part of me that *wanted* to hate that alligator—found its way back. I realized then that Abe had never intended to help me. He just needed some work done around his old shack and I was willing and gullible enough to trust him. I had struck a bargain with a grown-up. I had trusted him and I had been betrayed.

That would never happen again.

I stared at him hatefully. How I wanted to get back at him for what he had done to me…

"I thought you were different," I said. "But *you're* not different at all. You're just like all the rest."

I jammed my hands into my pockets and walked back to the truck. Mo trotted after me, whining softly. He nudged his snout against my hip and tried to lick my hand.

"Get outta here, Mo," I scowled and pushed him away.

But still he followed me, trying once more to lick my hand.

"Go on… *git*!" I pushed him a second time.

I started to climb into the back of the pickup where Buck was sitting, hunched forward and silent. Mo gave a soft, mournful howl and jumped up, putting his paws on my back.

Then my anger reached it's limit and I turned around. In that instant, all of the sorrow and rage and frustration and hate that had been building up inside me, found a target and exploded out of me like a shotgun blast. "I said… *GIT*!"

I slammed my fist across the side of Mo's head.

The old dog let out a yelp and backed away. I could see his eye twitching where I had struck him. He backed up a foot or two, whining, tilting his head and looking confused.

I'll remember that look as long as I live.

Part of me wanted to throw my arms around Mo and try to make him understand how sorry I was. But instead I just climbed into the back of the truck. Billy Ray turned the pickup around and drove us away. I could see Abe standing alone on his porch, watching us go. Mo followed behind us for a short way, then he turned around and trotted back to Abe. We drove back through the forest, and within seconds Abe's shack had disappeared from view.

29

Billy Ray took us home, and as we pulled up the driveway, Ma came out the kitchen door. I didn't look her in the face. I didn't want to see her expression. Billy Ray unloaded my bike and she thanked him for bringing me home. He said it wasn't a problem.

I went up to my room as quickly as I could and shut the door behind me. I had a million different emotions swirling around inside me at that moment. Part of me was sad because of the way I had treated Abe and Mo. But I was also nervous about having to face Ma and what kind of punishment she might be brewing.

Mostly though, I was angry.

I was angry at Rooster Mason and Ellis Woods for not believing me when I told them they had found the wrong alligator. If they would've believed me, I wouldn't have had to go looking for it myself in the first place. And I was angry at Buck for telling everyone that we had been out at Abe's place. If he'd just kept his mouth shut, no one would've ever found out. I was angry at Ma for sending Billy Ray to bring me home. She had ruined my chances of ever finding that alligator again after I had come so close! I was angry at the whole town for the way they treated old Abe. They wouldn't have raised nearly as much of a fuss if they weren't so suspicious of him. They just made up their minds about him without even bothering to find out the truth.

Most of all, I was angry at Abe. He had promised to help me and had gotten my hopes up. But in the end he broke his promise. He showed me he couldn't be trusted, just like everyone else in Silas.

A soft knock on my door brought me up from my thoughts.

I sighed. "What."

I was laying on my bed with my back facing the door. I heard it creak open and I could sense Ma was standing there. I didn't look at her or say anything and after a long pause she spoke.

"Are you angry?"

I could tell from her tone of voice that she didn't think I had as much of a right to be angry as she had. I sighed. I knew it was one of those questions that was specially designed to get us into an argument. If I said 'no', she'd accuse me of lying and tell me how angry she was with me. But if I said 'yes', she'd tell me I had no right to be angry at her, and then she'd tell me how angry she was with me. Either way, there was no escape from this inevitable conversation.

Unless I could throw her a curve ball…

"I don't know," I mumbled, grinning ever-so-slightly.

"You think this is funny?" she asked. It seemed like she was able to see that grin straight through the back of my head.

"No."

There was a long pause. Then she went on.

"Every morning you get up at dawn and you pack yourself a lunch and you tell me you're going fishing. And you and Buck are gone all day. You don't come back 'til supper time and you never even bring home a single fish."

I winced. How could I have overlooked such an obvious flaw in an otherwise perfect plan?

"And then I hear from—" she bit off her words. "From… *folks* that you and Buck have really been out in the swamp this whole time. And that you're hunting *alligators* with strangers—"

I rolled over to face her. "It wasn't no stranger, Ma. It was Abe Garner. And besides, you're the one who's always sayin' that we should—"

"I don't care!" she said, sharply. "I just lost my husband to an alligator not *three weeks* ago and I'm *not*—" Her voice cracked. She took a breath and continued evenly. "I am *not* going to lose you to one, as well."

I could see tears welling up in her eyes but they were still fierce and her jaw was firm. She shook her head and her voice softened.

"I don't want to lose you, too."

I rolled back to my stomach. "So am I grounded?"

"I haven't decided yet," she said. "But how can I trust you anymore?"

There was another long pause. Then she sat the foot of the bed. "I need your help, Jake. Even more so now."

She put her hand on my shoulder. I could sense by her touch and the long pause that there was bad news coming. I winced. What now? Things couldn't possibly get worse.

"Jake," she began, "the insurance company is not going to pay as much on your father's policy as I had expected. It's not going to be enough to cover all our bills. So I had to get a job."

I rolled back over to look at her again, but this time she turned away.

"We need the extra money," she said. "I'm going back to my old job at the nursing home up in Chase. It'll be afternoons and evenings mostly so I'll need you to keep an eye on Molly while I'm gone. I need you here at home, Jake."

In that instant, my world shrunk a thousand times. I was speechless. Things *had* gotten worse. With my chores in the mornings and now having to baby-sit in the afternoons and evenings, I wouldn't have any time left for myself. Not that it mattered. I had nowhere to go now anyway.

I sighed. "When do you start?"

"Monday," she replied. "Monday afternoon. I have to leave here by two-thirty and I probably won't be home til near midnight."

"Every day?"

"Most days, yeah."

I buried my head in my arms. So I *was* grounded after all. And this was my punishment. I'd have to be home by two-thirty every day. My summer vacation was evaporating right before my eyes.

Ma got up. "I'll make sure to have supper ready before I go. All you'll have to do is heat it up and do the dishes afterwards. And make sure Molly takes her baths—and you, too."

"I'm only *twelve*," I complained.

Ma nodded. "I know, but you'll have to be responsible. I can't afford a babysitter. It's either this, or we move closer to Aunt Lola—"

I groaned.

"—and I didn't think you'd like that too well. So you see, we have to help each other."

That night I lay in bed, staring at the ceiling. What had ever happened to the life I had just a few weeks ago? I closed my eyes and once again I could see me and Pa playing catch at the park that Saturday afternoon. We were laughing and kidding each other. But once again, I missed that last ball he threw and it bounced into the river. Once again, Pa went in to go get it…

It came down to that simple thing. Everything in our lives had changed so much just because I missed that ball. Pa was dead. Ma had to get a job. Now I would never get a chance to kill that alligator and no one would ever believe me. I wondered how things would've been different if Pa hadn't died in the first place. Our lives had changed so drastically all because I couldn't catch a softball.

Then I heard a tapping at my window and glanced at my clock. It was just after midnight. I looked out and found Buck sitting out on the roof.

"What're you doing here?" I whispered. "If your pa finds out—"

"You think my pa really cares where I am?" Buck whispered back. "He don't care about nothing except drinkin' his beer and drivin' his truck."

He climbed inside and we sat on the floor We just sat quietly for a few minutes until finally he spoke up.

"I was thinking… your ma will probably forget about all this in a week or so. We can sneak back out there again and—"

"Abe don't want us to come back no more," I said. "He told me. He said he won't take us back into the swamp either. He said not to come back."

Buck stared at me. "He *said* that?"

"I should've known," I scowled. "He got us to do all that work around his house. He wasn't gonna help us find that alligator. He was just using us is all."

Buck fell quiet for a moment. Then he sighed. "So what're you gonna do?"

I shrugged. "What *can* I do? And now I found out my ma has to go back to her old job at the nursing home. She said she's gonna be working from two-thirty til midnight and that I have to stay home and watch Molly while she's gone."

"*Two-thirty*?" Buck said, shaking his head. "That don't leave you much time for anything."

We sat there in the dark. It was a warm night and a breeze floated through the window, brushing aside the curtains.

Outside we could hear a soft chorus of crickets and an occasional dog barking in the distance. Neither of us said anything for a while.

I was sinking in my own self-pity. I felt like there was nothing in my life left to put my hope in any longer.

Then Buck looked up. "When does your ma start her job?"

"Monday."

Buck bit his lip and nodded to himself. "Then we don't have much time left."

I shook my head. "What're you talking about?"

"Do you still want to kill that gator?"

"Of course I do, but—"

"Then we gotta go tomorrow."

"*What*?" I whispered. "You wanna go back out there *tomorrow*? You're crazy!"

"No I ain't," Buck said. "My pa's got an old rifle he keeps out in the garage, and I know where he keeps the bullets. I used to take it out for target practice. I'm a pretty good shot too."

"But tomorrow's Sunday," I said. "I'm supposed to go to church—"

"Then we'll have to get an early start," Buck rubbed his hands together. "If we get started before dawn, we'll be long gone before anyone even knows we're missing."

I shook my head. This was crazy. I had to just stop listening to Buck. Even the best of his plans had a way of backfiring, and this was one of his worst.

"They'll send the whole town out looking for us. And then we'll *really* be in trouble."

"No we won't," Buck said. "Not when they see we killed that alligator. Then they'll finally believe us." He leaned close and whispered. "We'll be heroes."

I didn't reply to that. I couldn't. As much as I hated to admit it, that thought *did* appeal to me. Even though I was angry with most everyone in town, it would feel good to prove to them that I had been right all along. I would love to see the looks on their faces. I would give anything to hear them apologize, and admit they should have listened to me in the first place.

Especially Ma.

"So where are we gonna get a boat?" I challenged him.

Buck thought for a moment. "We'll take Abe's. If we get out there early enough, he'll still be asleep. He owes us anyway for all the work we've done out there. It won't even be like stealing."

"What if we get lost," I said. "We're not even sure where that boat house is."

"We know the general direction. Besides, a gator *that* big can't be too hard to find. And you can bring your compass along if you're scared of gettin' lost."

It was late and I knew I wasn't thinking too clearly but Buck seemed to have everything figured out. What had started out sounding like a crazy idea now actually seemed like it could really work. We didn't need old Abe along anyway. A grown-up would just want to take all the credit. But there was just one thing that bothered me…

"Ma's gonna kill me."

"No she won't," Buck said. "She's got too many other things on her mind to worry about *you* now. It's like how it is in my family. You got to look out for yourself. You got to make your *own* decisions."

Then he chuckled. "You're just like *me* now, Jake."

30

An early morning mist covered the black, murky water. Our boat glided over the surface without a sound as we drifted down the river. Buck sat at the bow and peered out into the gloom, clutching his pa's rifle close to his chest.

"I don't know," he whispered. "Maybe this wasn't such a good idea after all."

"It's too late to turn back now," I said.

It felt like we had been rowing for hours. The trees had grown in so thick around us, we couldn't see more than twenty or thirty feet ahead. We came around the trunk of a particularly big tree when Buck raised his hand.

"I think I see something up ahead," Buck said. "I can't quite tell…"

I peered over his shoulder. "What is it?"

"Just a little further."

I paddled a little more and Buck reached over the side, stretching to pluck something out of the water. He sat up and turned around, holding a small round object.

“A *softball*?” I said, staring at it in disbelief. How had a softball gotten out here?

At that moment, a shadow rose up behind Buck. It happened so quickly that I hardly had time to react. Cold, snake-like eyes glared at me through the mist and huge jaws opened. Water dripped from long, yellow teeth as the jaws clamped down hard on Buck’s arm. Buck screamed and reached out toward me with his free hand but I couldn’t move.

I wanted desperately to help him but I felt like I was frozen in my seat. With one twist of its head, the beast yanked Buck out of the boat and down into the water!

I tried to scream…

I sat up in bed, my heart racing and my body soaked in a cold sweat. It was the first nightmare I’d had in two weeks. I lay back and closed my eyes until my breathing slowed. It was almost four o’clock and still dark outside but I knew Buck was probably already on his way over.

I got dressed and eased open my bedroom window. Climbing out onto the roof, I made my way down the big oak tree. The stars still shown brightly and the moon was fat and full and hanging low above the line of trees to the west. The eastern horizon was just beginning to brighten with the first, faint trace of dawn. I reached the ground and found Buck already waiting for me on his bike. He had his pa’s rifle wrapped in a towel and tied across the handlebars.

“It’s about time,” Buck whispered. “I thought I was gonna have to come up there and drag you outta bed.”

I nodded toward the gun. “You got it, huh.”

"Yep," he said and pulled out a small cardboard box from the pocket of his jacket. "Found a whole box of bullets, too."

I snuck into the barn and wheeled my bike out. I looked back at the house and took a deep breath.

"I don't know about this," I said, as the seriousness of what we were about to do started to sink in. "I'm gonna get in a lot of trouble."

Buck chuckled. "Don't go gettin' chicken on me now, Jake."

We rode off down the driveway and into town. The streets were empty and all the buildings and storefronts were filled with shadows. It was like riding through a ghost town.

All the while, I kept thinking that I still had time to change my mind. I'd be able to get back home without Ma ever knowing that I had been gone.

But instead, we continued following the highway out of town and turned off on the gravel road, riding as fast as we could. By the time we reached the dirt road that led out to Abe's cabin, the sky was turning from purple to gray. We could barely see the path in front of us as we road through the woods. We hid our bikes in some bushes just up the path from his shack and crouched behind a tree at the edge of the clearing to see if there was any sign of Abe or Mo around.

The whole place was dark and still.

We crept out onto the dock, untied Abe's boat, climbed inside, and quietly pushed off. We let ourselves drift away down the river before we started rowing, so that we'd make as little noise as possible. The water was as black and murky as it had been in my dream. The trees loomed up around us like giant silhouettes in the mist, their gnarled, moss-covered branches reaching out toward us from the fog.

Buck sat at the bow with his pa's rifle loaded and ready beside him. I sat in the rear and as we glided down the river, I found myself fighting back all sorts of nervous thoughts that had come over me. Thoughts of what Ma would do when we got back. In all my life I had never done anything this deliberately disobedient and I couldn't even imagine what kind of punishment would be in store for me. More than this, as I peered into the water, I half-expected to see some gigantic black shape moving around beneath the surface. We drifted past the spot in the river where we had set our trap and I grew even more uneasy. This had been the exact place that we had nearly captured the monster a few days before, and I wondered if it could still be lurking somewhere nearby.

We continued on deeper into the swamp.

Before long, the river widened and we couldn't tell where the water ended and the shore began. We passed by the twisted trunk of a fallen tree sticking out of the water. In the fog, it resembled the head of a sea-monster, and looked like it could come alive any moment. But it remained quiet and motionless as we passed by.

After a while, we came to another fallen tree. It was at this point that the river divided into two branches. To the left, it narrowed and curled around a bend, while to the right, the trees grew thicker and gloomier than ever. In fact, in that direction it appeared as though the whole swamp had stretched itself out over everything and no dry land was anywhere to be seen.

"What d'you think?" Buck asked as he peered in both directions. "Which way?"

I knew which way I would've rather gone, but I also knew which direction the old boathouse was most likely in. I nodded off to the right. "That way."

Buck looked back at me and raised an eyebrow. "I was afraid you were gonna say that."

So we headed off deeper into the swamp and soon found ourselves drifting between wide tree trunks and around big patches of reeds and mud. The water was covered with a thick coat of green scum. At times it looked almost like dry land, but it would part in front of us as we glided through and come together again directly behind us, leaving almost no trace that we had ever even passed by.

I had brought my compass along with me to keep track of the direction we were heading. Although I couldn't see much of the sky through all the trees, I could tell it was growing brighter and the mist had thinned out a bit. The steady drone of insects hummed in our ears along with the echoes of birds calling and bullfrogs croaking in the distance. Every once in a while we would hear another sound. A deep, growling hiss that came from somewhere in the fog and sent shivers down our backs.

We rowed for another half hour or so before pausing again beside a thick cypress tree that rose up from a patch of reeds. I checked my watch. It was almost six o'clock. Before long, Ma would be waking up to make breakfast. Then she would come up to my room to wake me up for church and find out I was gone.

I suddenly had a guilty feeling in the pit of my stomach. She would be frantic. The first thing she'd do would be to call the Rooster again, and they'd start combing the whole river for us. I shook my head and sighed. Part of me knew I was going to be in big trouble. Ma would ground me for the rest of the summer.

But the other part didn't care. I had to find that alligator and kill it. No one else but Buck seemed to understand that. I *had* to kill it. And with Ma starting her job the next day, I knew I would never have another chance. I had to do it now no matter how much trouble I'd get in because of it.

"We'd better hurry up," I said. "We ain't got much time."

Buck nodded and we started rowing again.

By this time we were deep into the swamp, well beyond any point that Abe had ever shown us before. We were like sailors exploring some uncharted sea. The fact that we had no idea how far we would have to go made me pretty uncomfortable. Every time we rounded a bend we strained to see any sign of the boat house, but each turn just led us farther into the swamp. And the farther in we went, the gloomier it looked.

Without any better option, we continued in the same direction Abe had pointed whenever he told us about the boat house. I hadn't counted on it being that hard to find or taking that long. I guess I had thought we would just come across it sooner or later as long as we kept on in the right direction. But out here, the swamp seemed to go on in every direction.

Suddenly, Buck sat up and pointed ahead. "Hey! I think that's it!"

I could see the shadowy outline of a small structure in the mist up ahead of us. It was stranded several yards from shore and as we got closer, we could see it was mostly a rotting, wooden frame rising up out of the murky water. Moss hung down from the roof, and vines had grown up over the walls.

A rickety dock jutted out twenty feet or so from the main section. Cattails and reeds had grown in thick around the whole area, making it look creepier than I had imagined.

We pulled up to the dock, tied the boat off and tested the wooden planks to make sure they'd support us. They were soft and creaked quite a bit but they held our weight well enough.

As we looked around, we could see that the boat house itself was nothing more than a small shack with just enough room to store one boat inside. The wooden doors across the front were rotted and the hinges and locks were all brown with rust.

A narrow deck ran the length of the shack and there was a small doorway on one side. We peeked inside but the place was deserted and looked like it had been for a long time. Light streamed in between the slats in the walls. It was filled with spider webs and dust. A fishing net hung on the far wall with an old life-preserver next to it. The whole place smelled like a musty attic filled with dead fish.

Buck wrinkled his nose. "It stinks in here."

We followed the deck around back and scanned the area. Weeds had grown thick along the shoreline where Abe had said he'd seen the giant gator lying in the mud. Maybe this was where it lived. Maybe it was hiding out there in the reeds right now. It could be anywhere, I thought, and I suddenly had the feeling that we were being watched. A chill ran down my spine and I rubbed my arms. "This place gives me the creeps."

"You ain't gettin' chicken, are ya?" Buck said.

"No," I said. "I just feel like we ain't alone out here, is all."

No sooner had I said those words, we heard a sound that made us both freeze. The low purr of a motor came to us from somewhere in the fog.

A boat was coming.

31

We stared at each other for a terrified moment. Who would be out here at this hour? Had they sent a search party after us already? Had they discovered that we were missing so soon? That was impossible. It wasn't even seven o'clock.

Then we heard voices echoing through the fog. I couldn't tell what they were saying but they were definitely getting closer!

Buck turned pale. "Who is it? No one even knows we're out here."

I strained to listen. "Sounds like they're coming from that way—from out of the swamp."

"C'mon," Buck said. "We'd better get outta here."

We climbed back into the boat and shoved off, but the sound of the motor was much louder now. I glanced over my shoulder and spotted a large, dark shape coming toward us from out of the mist.

"Wait," I whispered. "They'll see us! Get behind the boathouse."

We paddled around to the side of the boathouse and pulled the boat up close into the reeds where we would be hidden from view. We waited, peering through the slats in the walls. The boat drew closer and I strained to see who would possibly be this far out in the swamp this early in the morning.

By now, I could tell it was a pontoon boat with three men sitting underneath a canopy, draped with mosquito netting. I couldn't see their faces at all. Two of them looked to be pretty good-sized and the third one, sitting at the front, was a smaller fellow.

Buck and I crouched down in the boat, hoping they would just pass by and continue up the river. But soon it was clear they were headed right for the boathouse.

They shut off their motor as they drew up to the dock. The skinny man climbed down and tied off the boat. From my viewpoint, peeking through the slats in the walls, I could only see their legs as they all climbed onto the dock. I could hear them muttering to each other, but I still couldn't make out what they were saying. One of the bigger men was carrying a rifle. He walked over to the door of the boathouse and peered inside. We ducked down, holding our breath and hoping he wouldn't see our boat through the slats in the walls. We lay flat in the bottom for several seconds until we felt it was safe to sit up.

I peeked through the slats once more and saw that the three of them were standing back out on the dock near their boat. I breathed a short sigh of relief. Maybe they had just come by to look around. Maybe they had seen the old boathouse and were curious is all, and now they'd be on their way again. I leaned forward to see if I could catch a glimpse of their faces. I pulled myself up and peered through a higher slat. One of the bigger men suddenly turned in my direction and I gasped when I saw his face—

Ellis Woods!

His wide-brimmed hat was pulled down low over his forehead but I could see his face clearly. Stubble covered his jaw and his clothes looked wrinkled and stained. Then I recognized the other two men as well. Max Finney and Morris Boggs—his two hired hands that we had met at the festival. They looked to be arguing about something. Finney, the smaller man, had a disgusted look on his face.

"*Three days*," he scowled as he took a swig from a canteen. "We been out here for *three days straight*, and we ain't seen a blasted thing!"

"It's here," Ellis said. "Believe me, it's out here somewhere. I can feel it."

Finney grunted, "*Feel* it? You dragged us out here in the middle of nowhere and all you got to go on is a *feeling*?"

"I didn't say it'd be easy," Ellis growled. "And I'm not paying you to give me your opinions so keep your eyes open and your mouth shut."

Morris Boggs scratched his head. "But it's been two weeks since it killed that fella. It's probably miles away by now. Why don't we just wait 'til we hear if it kills someone else and then start trackin' it fresh again. Wouldn't that be easier than searchin' through the whole swamp?"

Ellis spun around to face Boggs. His eyes flared with anger. "I can't afford to wait until it kills someone else you idiot. I can't risk having any more witnesses!

We've got to find it, now—*before* it kills again and folks start spreading more rumors."

Boggs looked confused. "I ain't no idiot."

"No, you're a bloody genius." Ellis snorted and shook his head. He paced the dock, cradling his rifle and muttering to himself.

My mouth went dry as I listened to their conversation. They were still looking for the alligator! The last time I had seen Ellis Woods was on the dock behind the hardware store, standing proudly in front of the gator he'd killed. He had convinced everyone that it was the one that had attacked Pa. But now it sounded like he knew it *wasn't* the right one. And he had known it all along.

But I didn't get it. How did he know? Something was very wrong. It was as if the pieces of a giant puzzle were slowly starting to fall in place but I couldn't quite figure out what the whole picture was.

Buck frowned and whispered. "I don't get it."

"They're hunting the alligator too," I said. "The same one we're after."

"I thought he didn't believe you."

I shook my head. "I don't know. I think all that was just an…"

Buck's face suddenly turned white. He stared at me with his eyes wide and his mouth open. I was about to ask him what was wrong when I realized that he wasn't staring *at* me. He was looking *past* me, at the deck that ran along the back of the boathouse.

"Wull now," a voice behind me said. "Look-it what we have here."

32

I turned around and saw Ellis Woods scowling down the barrel of the rifle he had pointed right at us. He stood at the edge of the deck, and for a moment, he looked like he was going to shoot us. But then his scowl faded and he lowered his rifle.

"It's you." He nodded to himself and grunted. "I might've known you'd find your way out here sooner or later. What exactly d'you think you're doin' here?"

"We're just fishing," I said. My mind had gone blank and I couldn't think of any other excuse.

Ellis chewed on the inside of his cheek and stood with one hand on his hip and the other cradling his gun. He stared at us for a long while, as if he was trying to figure out how much of his conversation we had overheard. "Mighty long way just to go fishing," he said at last.

I felt myself squirming. "It ain't that far."

"Besides," he added, nodding at Buck's rifle. "What kind of fish were you expecting to catch with *that*?"

"Ain't no law against us bein' out here," Buck said, defiantly.

"No," Ellis snorted, "but I bet if your folks knew you were here, you'd be in trouble."

My mind raced for an answer. "Uh…"

Ellis narrowed his eyes. "You're still looking for that alligator, aren't you?"

I didn't know what to say. I couldn't tell him about our deal with Abe or how we had nearly caught the creature in our trap. But I also didn't want to look like I was lying.

"How long have you boys been hiding back here?" Ellis went on.

I looked down and shrugged. The back of my neck started prickling again. I didn't want to make him angry by not answering him, but I also didn't want him to know that we had been eavesdropping either.

Ellis sighed and shook his head. "No matter. Tie your boat off. I want to have a talk with you two."

For a moment, I thought of trying to escape but I knew we wouldn't get very far in a rowboat. And if Ellis didn't shoot us first, he'd certainly be able to catch us in his boat. I started to feel sick and wondered what he was going to do with us. And I started wishing I had never listened to Buck's plan.

With no better alternative at that moment, we tied off our boat and climbed onto the dock, standing there sheepishly as the three of them stared at us long and hard.

"You boys had anything to eat?" Ellis asked, finally. "You look hungry."

My stomach had been growling earlier but now it was all tied in knots. "No."

Ellis chuckled and motioned for us to follow him. "C'mon, you must be starving. You've probably been up since before dawn to make it out here this early."

Buck and I exchanged glances. I guess we both figured if he was going to shoot us, he would have done it by now. So we followed him onto his boat. The deck was cluttered with piles of fishing gear and other equipment and the whole boat looked even more run down now that we could see it up close.

Ellis set his rifle against the steering panel and opened a large cooler. He dug through it and pulled out two sandwiches, wrapped in waxpaper.

"Here you go." he held them out to us, but we just stared at them.

"Don't worry, they're not poisoned."

We took the sandwiches and Ellis drew up three rusted lawnchairs underneath the canopy. He flopped into one of the chairs and motioned for us to join him. "Have a seat."

We sat down while Finney and Boggs kept their distance, sitting on a large crate near the front of the boat with their arms folded.

I took a bite of my sandwich. It was ham and Swiss cheese with some kind of brown mustard that made my nose sting. Ellis pulled out a bottle of liquor and took a long drink, wiping his mouth with the back of his hand.

"So what makes you think your mysterious giant alligator really exists? What makes you so sure it wasn't the one I killed?"

"I'm *not* sure." I chose my words carefully.

Ellis snorted. "Oh I dunno, you sounded pretty sure that day at the dock. And you must've been sure enough to come all the way out here looking for it."

I swallowed a mouthful of sandwich but it felt dry and hard without anything to drink. "Like I told you, the one I saw was bigger than the one you killed. A *lot* bigger."

Ellis nodded. "So you got a good look at it, did you?"

"Pretty good, yeah."

Ellis stared out at the water. His eyes were sort of glazed over, like he was extremely tired, which he probably was. Or like he'd had too much to drink, which he probably had. Then the corner of his mouth raised a little with a grim smile as he sighed.

"Well, you're right, Jake. That gator I brought back wasn't what killed your father."

I frowned. "But *you* knew it all along."

"Yes."

"Why did you do it then? Why did you lie?"

Ellis still had a faraway look in his eyes and he swished the bottle gently. "I had to protect something. Something very important to me. Everyone in town was out hunting for that animal after your father was killed. And I couldn't risk someone else getting killed. Or even worse, one of them killing it."

"Why not?"

"Because it's worth too much to me."

I could feel my anger rising. *Worth too much?* This animal's life was more important to him than four human lives? More than my father's? And more than that, he been lying to everyone to try to keep it alive.

"But…" my jaw clenched and I shook my head. "That alligator killed my father. We have to kill it. It deserves to die."

"That was no alligator that killed your father, Jake." Ellis grunted and took another drink. "What killed your father would make that gator I brought back look like an iguana."

33

I stared at Ellis in disbelief. But he just sat there with no real expression on his face, almost like he was in a trance or something. No emotion at all. I struggled to make sense out of what he was saying.

"What're you talking about?"

"He's just drunk," Buck scowled.

Ellis chuckled. "Yeah, I am a little drunk."

"And you're talkin' too much!" Finney growled, glaring at Ellis.

Ellis just snorted. "Quit your nagging, Max. You're starting to get on my nerves."

Finney turned to Boggs, muttering something under his breath and Ellis chuckled. "Max worries like a mother hen. I honestly don't think he's happy unless he's got something to fuss over."

"What do you mean it wasn't an alligator?" I persisted.

"What killed your father was a twenty-four foot African crocodile," Ellis said. "Not an alligator."

"What difference does that make?" Buck said, sounding annoyed.

Ellis shifted in his seat. "Oh, it makes quite a bit of difference, actually. They're two very different animals. See, your North American alligators are usually pretty timid They don't normally attack people unless they're provoked. They're used to preying on smaller animals so they tend to shy away from humans and larger game."

He took another sip from his bottle and wiped his mouth. "But a crocodile…" he shook his head. "Wull now, that's another matter. See, crocs are bigger and more aggressive animals. Some of the big Nile lizards can grow to be sixteen, eighteen feet long, and they're used to bringing down big game like zebras and wildebeests. They're not so easily put off by humans. We're nothing but food to them, just like everything else."

My head was spinning. "So how did an African crocodile get to Silas?"

Ellis took a deep breath and gazed upward. "Wull that's a long story."

"And one we ain't got time for," Finney scowled. "Why don't you just go to the sheriff and make a full confession!"

Ellis glared back at Finney. "It killed his father, Max. The boy at least deserves an explanation."

Ellis turned back to me and his expression softened a bit. "I was right around your age when I saw my first crocodile. I was out fishing with my father when it swam right past our boat. It was magnificent! At least twelve feet long. From that day on, I was hooked. I started collecting all sorts of reptiles. Drove me mum bonkers. My dream was to someday open up my own reptile zoo.

Crocs, Komodos, alligators. The bigger the better. I studied zoology at college and worked at a few different crocodile farms down in Australia."

Then he sighed and shook his head. "But things didn't work out too well for me so I decided to come to America and open up a reptile park over here. I sold everything I owned to buy *Gator World.* But after two years, I was going bankrupt. I have a good location, good stock—everything I needed for success, except one thing: a *main attraction.* You know, something *really* special that would bring folks in. Something they'll pay money to see!"

He took another drink. "Then about a year ago, a friend of mine told me about this giant croc he'd seen down in the Congo. He said the locals called it *Mto Ibilisi,* The River Devil. Said it was the biggest, most aggressive crocodile he'd ever seen in his life. He said it would attack anything that moved. It seemed to kill just for the joy of killing."

His face brightened and his eyes gleamed. "I knew that was my ticket! If I could capture that animal and bring it back to *Gator World*, it'd pack the people in. So I invested every last dime I had to take an expedition down the Congo River and find that crocodile."

He wiped the back of his neck with a bandana. "And we found it all right. I'd never seen anything like it in my life! It was incredible! A massive, twenty-four foot killing machine. Unbelievably strong and quick. I lost two men just trying to capture it. It bit through one fellow's leg like a stick of butter. It was the most magnificent animal I'd ever seen in my life!"

Buck looked irritated. "And you brought it back *here*?"

Ellis nodded. "Oh, I had to pull a few of strings to get it into the country. He was going to be my star attraction. I called him *Goliath.* And he was going to save my park."

I felt dizzy but I began to understand, and I didn't like what I was hearing. "So what happened?" I asked. "How'd it get loose?"

Ellis tightened his lips. "I had… *underestimated* his strength. He broke out of his holding pen and disappeared just a few days after I got him here. Luckily, I had kept it all a secret up til then, so no one ever knew what had happened."

"When was that?" Buck asked.

"Earlier this spring," Ellis said. "I've been trying to track him ever since but it hasn't been easy. There's a lot of rivers and swamps in these parts that're all interconnected. It hasn't been easy at all. After I heard about what happened to Jake's father, I figured Goliath had followed the river all the way down from Bilford."

"So you knew all along that it killed my pa." I said.

"I was pretty sure. Especially after I saw how badly he was—" Ellis stopped and bit his lip. "I was pretty sure, yeah."

"And you killed one of your other alligators and made everyone think it had killed my pa?" It was all clear to me now. All of it except for one thing.

"What about his watch? Ma told me you found his watch inside—"

Ellis nodded. "I talked the sheriff into letting me see your father's body. Or what was left of it. I told him it'd be a good idea if he wanted my *professional* opinion. I managed to lift his watch when no one was looking."

I felt nauseous. "You… you *stole* his watch?"

"I *had* to do it, Jake. You understand that, don't you?"

As I looked up at him, I could feel the blood drain from my face. I still couldn't believe what I was hearing. This was the man everyone thought had been a hero. But he was just a fraud and a liar—and a murderer as well! He was trying to pass himself off as some kind of hero. He had even told Ma that he had killed that other—

Then I realized there was more to all of this than I had thought. That giant puzzle had finally come into focus to form a picture I never even knew was there.

And Pa's death was just one piece.

"It killed that girl up in Chase too, didn't it?"

Ellis looked down. "When I first heard about that little girl, I was sick inside. I knew it was Goliath. I got into town as soon as I could. I had to work quick to stop the locals from starting up a search party there too. I couldn't risk them finding him. It would've ruined me."

"But why?" I demanded. "Why didn't you just *tell* the sheriff when it first got loose? Why did you keep it a secret? You could've gotten plenty of help to track it down."

Ellis shook his head. "They never would've let me take him alive. And they'd start asking too many questions. Let's just say I had my reasons for wanting to keep this quiet."

He leaned forward and lowered his voice. "You've got to believe me, Jake. I never intended for anyone to get hurt. But I've got everything invested in that animal. I can't let anyone else find out what's happened. It'd ruin me, Jake. Everything I've worked for my whole life… I'd lose everything."

He leaned back and his eyes went cold. "I'm not going to let that happen, Jake."

He just sat there, looking at me without any expression. His eyes were as cold as a snake's, without sorrow or regret or any emotion at all.

Then something came over me that I couldn't control. I could feel my anger boiling in the center of my chest and suddenly it exploded without warning.

I flew out of my chair and lunged straight at Ellis. I saw a brief look of surprise on his face as I swung my arms with all the hate and anger that had been building up inside me. I felt my fist connect with his jaw, sending sharp jolts of pain through my wrist. But I didn't care. At that moment, I hated Ellis Woods with all the hate in the world and I knew I would've killed him if I could have.

Ellis lurched backward as I got ready to swing again. But before I could land a second punch, I felt something crash into the side of my head. A bright flash of light streaked across my vision, and then everything went black.

34

"Jake."

Somewhere off in the darkness, a voice whispered my name.

"*Jake*."

I don't know how long it had been calling me but at some point I began to get irritated. I tried to answer. *What do you want*?

Then I heard a second voice that sounded closer that the first. "Mmmuffudduffummel."

The first voice whispered again. "Jake… you okay?"

I tried to turn my head but it felt like it weighed a thousand pounds. I couldn't move it at all. I tried to answer again. *What*?

"Mmmmmmmud?"

"Jake… *wake up*!"

Bolts of pain shot through my skull as I groaned and forced my eyelids half open. All I could see were gray blurs of light and shadows.

"Jake," the voice whispered. It was Buck.

"Mmmmm," was all I could manage to say.

Slowly, the blurs came into focus. Clouds. I was lying on my back, staring up at the sky. But the cloud bank looked a sickly green color and seemed to bulge and sway in a very odd motion. Then I realized I was actually lying facedown on the deck, watching the sky's reflection in the murky water.

I could hear the muddy *blah blah* of voices in the background, and Buck was nearby, still whispering to me. "C'mon Jake. *Please* wake up."

I rolled onto my side. Buck was hunkered down next to me with a very concerned look on his face.

"Whuhhapnd?" I mumbled. My jaw felt too stiff and sore to talk clearly and my skull was still pounding.

Buck shook his head. "Ellis belted you a good one upside your head. I thought he killed you at first."

By now, my memory was starting to come back. Ellis Woods had told us how he had brought some giant crocodile over from Africa and how it had gotten loose in the river. It had killed Sarah Mae Hatcher up in Chase and Pa as well. I remembered feeling so angry that all I wanted to do was kill Ellis for what he'd done.

Buck peered over his shoulder and then back at me. "They're goin' out after the crocodile again. And I think they're gonna take us with 'em this time."

I struggled to sit up. My head had cleared, even though it still felt like someone was pounding inside it with a hammer. And I could feel my cheek and my right eye had swollen up.

I looked around. We were sitting at the back of the pontoon boat, which was still tied up to the dock of the old boat house. Ellis, Finney and Boggs stood at the front, talking in hushed tones. Finney looked upset about something and Ellis seemed angry, too. He whispered harshly and pointed a finger in Finney's face.

Buck looked worried. "What're we gonna do?"

"I dunno," I mumbled. I couldn't think straight anymore.

Then Ellis Woods came back and stood over us with his hands on his hips. "Sorry about your jaw," he grunted. "I didn't mean to hit you quite that hard but you sort of took me by surprise."

I rubbed my eye. "What're you gonna do with us?"

Ellis shook his head and scratched the back of his neck. "Well, I haven't figured that out yet. I can't very well let you go at the moment. Although, I doubt anyone'll believe you if you tell them about us. But still, I can't risk that. At least not until I find Goliath. So until then, I suggest you sit tight and keep your mouths shut."

Max Finney grunted and scratched his jaw. "A lot of good *that'll* do," he scowled. "Why don't you just let me and Boggs take care of 'em like I said."

"Shut up, Max!" Ellis snapped. "I told you we're gonna handle this *my* way. Besides, they're not gonna cause us any trouble." He glared down at us. "Are you, boys?"

"No sir," we both said quickly.

Finney came over and leaned his thin, leathery face close to us. "You better *not*!" he growled. His hot breath smelled like liverwurst and beer. "Not if you know what's good for you."

Ellis climbed into the stool behind the steering wheel and started up the engine. The motor sputtered to life and spat out a blue cloud of exhaust.

Boggs untied the boat and Ellis pulled back on the throttle, moving us backward, away from the dock. Then he spun the wheel and swung the front end around until we faced the opposite direction. He pushed the lever forward again, and the motor raced for a second, then sputtered and died.

Ellis tried the key again. The motor chugged several times but still wouldn't start. He pounded the wheel and glared at Boggs. "I thought you said you fixed this thing."

Boggs shrugged. "It's an old engine. Whutch you expect?"

"I expected you to fix it!" Ellis scowled.

Boggs slid a tool box out from under a tarp and squatted down beside the motor. He unlatched the cover and peered inside, scratching his jaw.

Meanwhile, the boat continued to drift further away from the dock and out into deeper water. I glanced at my watch. It was nearly eight o'clock. Ma would be awake, and had probably realized I was missing by now. Maybe she had already called the sheriff. Maybe they were even out searching for us this very minute. I strained to listen for the sounds of other boats in the distance.

Then the deck shuddered as the pontoons scraped against something solid under the water. I could feel us tilting slightly to one side.

Boggs looked up from the motor. "What was that?"

Ellis leaned over the railing and peered into the water. "We're hung up on a log or something."

We were stuck about twenty yards out from the dock. Ellis reached under one of the tarps and produced a long wooden pole, capped with a hook one end. He thrust it down into the water, poking and prodding around in several spots beneath the pontoon.

"I can't feel anything down there."

He moved to the other side of the boat and dragged the hook along the bottom there as well. I could hear him muttering and cursing under his breath. Then it looked as if the pole ran up against something solid.

"There it is." He poked around the object. "Yep… feels like a big log."

He jammed the pole down and pushed against the log to see if he could pry us loose, but the boat wouldn't budge. He thrust it down a second time, with both hands, but still couldn't free us. Finally, he turned to Finney.

"Get over here and give me a han—"

Before he could finish, the pole tore loose from his grasp—as if it had come alive—and slapped down hard into the water.

The whole deck rocked as the foamy surface of the swamp churned and bubbled. A few seconds later, three splintered pieces of wood bobbed back up to the surface.

Ellis steadied himself. "What the—"

He stopped as the deck vibrated with a hollow scraping sound. Something was moving underneath us.

Something very big.

I peered over the side as a huge, black shape moved slowly out from underneath us, scraping against the pontoon as it emerged. It took several seconds for the thing to clear the boat and when it did, we could see it was enormous! A gigantic shadow gliding under the murky water, weaving slowly from side to side.

Ellis stood over us, staring at it like he was in some sort of a trance. His eyes were wide and he began to laugh. "There you are," he said, as if he thought the thing in the water could hear him. "I knew you were close by."

Several yards away, the water bubbled and a long row of thick, leathery ridges poked up through the surface. At first, it moved away from us, toward the boat house. But then it made a wide arc and circled back toward us.

"Max!" Ellis shouted. "Get the rope, he's coming back around!"

Finney dug out a bundle of rope from under the tarp and tied one end to a metal bracket bolted to the front of the deck.

Ellis opened a large, leather case and produced an odd-looking rifle with a scope mounted on top of a long, polished barrel. He opened a second, smaller case that contained what looked to be several tranquilizer darts.

"Get that motor running!" he shouted to Boggs.

"I'm workin' on it," Boggs muttered, wiping the sweat from his forehead.

I turned back to see the crocodile gliding toward us through the water. It was so big it didn't even look real, but more like some sea monster from a horror movie. Finney positioned himself at the railing with several yards of the rope in his hands. He had fashioned a loop in the free end. The rest of it lay coiled at his feet.

Ellis finished loading a dart into the gun and slung his arm through the shoulder strap. "Get ready, Max!"

I tried to get a better view as the crocodile came up along side the boat. It raised its massive head out of the water and opened its jaws in deep growl. Its pink tongue lay like a thick slab of ham behind its sharp, yellow teeth. Its mouth was big enough to swallow me whole, and I caught the stink of rotten fish as it passed by.

I couldn't believe the size of it! I had never been this close before. It was longer than the whole pontoon boat and as big around as the trunk of the oak tree in our front yard!

Finney leaned over and dropped the loop into the water just as the croc swam by. It crashed into the side of the pontoon and snapped at the rope, catching it in its mouth. Its jaws clamped shut and towed the line along with it.

The rope tore loose out of Finney's grasp, nearly pulling him over the railing. He stumbled backward and got his leg tangled in the coil at his feet. As the crocodile swam away, the rope tightened around Finney's leg, pinning him against the rail. He grimaced and swore.

Ellis moved forward to get a better shot. He lined the animal up in his sights, but before he could fire the dart, we heard a loud *crack* as part of the wooden railing broke away and the croc yanked Finney over the side, into the water!

35

I watched the crocodile swim away, dragging Max Finney along with it. I could see him struggling to untangle himself from the rope. He popped up once and managed a brief, gurgled cry before the croc yanked him under again.

The line pulled tight against the metal bracket in the deck, and the whole boat lurched forward, knocking me off balance. The rope strained for a moment, then snapped and fell limp into the water. An eerie silence engulfed us as Ellis crouched at the edge of the deck, scanning the river.

Finney's head popped up again, thirty feet ahead of us, coughing and gasping for breath. He flailed about, trying to get loose from the rope. His eyes buldged out from his pale face making him look like a giant white toad in the water. He finally managed to get free and started swimming furiously back to the boat.

Just as he started paddling, a huge black shape appeared in the water, gliding after him like a torpedo.

"You'd better hurry up, Max," Ellis called out. "He's right behind you!"

Finney's face held a mask of terror. "Help me!"

"Max!" Boggs shouted. "Hurry up!"

"Shoot it!" Finney screamed, choking on a mouthful of water.

"Come on Max." Ellis said, calmly. "You're almost here…"

"*Shoot it*!"

Boggs grabbed one of the rifles and took aim, but Ellis shoved the barrel away as the shot fired. The two men wrestled for control until Ellis slammed the butt of the rifle up into the bigger man's jaw. Ellis yanked the gun away, but it slipped out his own grasp and fell over the side into the water.

Dazed by the blow, Boggs staggered back and tumbled to the deck.

"*Help me!*" Finney screamed once more. He was only a few yards away from the boat and I could see his eyes, wide with terror as he reached out.

In that instant his face look just like Pa's…

Then the giant lizard was upon him. It raised its great bulk up out of the water and crashed back down on him like a cat pouncing on a field mouse. Its jaws opened wide and, with a deep growl, it clamped down hard across Finney's waist. He disappeared instantly beneath the murky water, followed by the massive back and tail of the crocodile as it submerged. Its leathery ridges passed by like traincars, curving down and disappearing into the black water. The boat rocked as the swamp churned and foamed beneath us for several seconds.

Then the water grew calm, the boat settled, and we never saw Max Finney again.

I stared at the water, unable to think or move. I couldn't believe what I had just seen. Ellis paced along the edge of the deck, peering into the river but there was no sign of Finney or the crocodile anywhere. It was as if they had both disappeared right underneath us.

"W-where is he?" I stammered. "What happened?"

"It took him under for a death roll," Ellis said, grimly. "There's nothing we can do."

"Did it—did it *eat* him?" Buck looked like he was going to be sick.

Ellis shook his head. "More'n likely it has a lair nearby. Some place secluded, where it can keep the body until it gets hungry again."

My stomach turned. "Keep the body?"

Morris Boggs picked himself up off the deck. Blood trickled from the corner of his mouth and he gave Ellis an icy stare. "You let that thing kill Max!"

Ellis wheeled around and glared at him. "Don't *ever* pull a stunt like that again!" he growled. "I didn't come through all this just to end up with a dead crocodile!"

Boggs shook his head. "You… you just *stood* there and let him die!"

"Max knew the risks," Ellis said. "You both did! He got careless and he paid the price for it. Now get that motor fixed or we'll all end up the same way."

The two men stared at each other for several moments Finally, Morris Boggs lowered his gaze, turned around and went back to work on the motor.

Ellis squatted down at the front of the boat and began drawing in what was left of the rope. He glanced back at us and shook his head. "Don't feel sorry for Max.

He knew what he was getting himself into when he agreed to work for me. You two should just be glad you didn't run across that croc while you were out in that little boat of yours or else you'd be dead by now, too."

He drew in the last few feet of the rope and inspected the end carefully. Then he held it out to us and we could see that it had been sliced neatly through.

"This ain't no petting zoo gator we're looking for," he said. "It's a twenty-four foot, African crocodile. A perfect killing-machine."

He stood and paced along the edge of the deck, peering out across the water. I imagine he was trying to find some trace of where his prize croc had gone off to. I couldn't see anything out there, though. The whole swamp was as still as death. No birds called and no insects buzzed around.

The air felt damp and heavy like it always did right before a summer storm. The sky had been gray and overcast all morning but now a purple wall of clouds had rolled in. Ellis noticed it as well.

He took off his hat and wiped his forehead with the back of his arm. "We're gonna get some rain." He turned back to Boggs. "How much longer til that motor's fixed."

"It's done," Boggs grunted. His eyes still seemed distant and cold. I couldn't see any emotion in them at all. He clamped the cover back on the engine. Then he went to the steering panel and turned the key. The motor chugged to life again, spewing out a steady stream of blue exhaust. But after a few moments, it was running smoothly.

Ellis pointed ahead, deeper into the swamp. "He must have gone off that way."

Boggs didn't argue or question him. He just pushed the throttle forward, spun the wheel and headed us deeper into the gray mist of the swamp. Off in the distance came the low rumble of thunder.

The swamp widened as we ventured further into it. Boggs steered us between gnarled tree trunks and patches of mud and reeds. Behind us, the shadowy silhouette of the boathouse disappeared in the mist. Ellis paced across the front of the boat with the tranquilizer gun in his grasp, peering into the gloom.

I watched him closely. His face looked grim—jaw clenched, lips tight—not at all like the man we had met at the festival just a few weeks before. I wondered what he must've been thinking at that time. It seemed the only thing driving him now was the goal of catching his crocodile and making money. I wondered if he was thinking about the three people his monster had killed since it had gotten loose. I wondered if he felt sorry for them, or if he even had a conscience at all.

The clouds grew thicker and the swamp got so dark it looked almost like dusk. Thunder rumbled overhead and the first heavy drops of rain pelted me in the face. Then in the distance came a rushing sound, like a small brook somewhere off in the woods. The sound grew steadily louder and before we knew it, we found ourselves in the middle of a downpour. Buck and I hunkered down under the canopy, trying to keep dry. Ellis stood on the deck, oblivious to the rain. It beat down on his hat and poured off the brim in tiny rivers onto his back and shoulders.

Lightning skipped across the clouds and lit up the swamp in wild flashes, followed closely by a loud, rolling *booms* that shook our ribs.

Before long, Ellis raised his hand and motioned for Boggs to stop the boat. He joined us back under the canopy, shaking his head. "We'll have to wait it out," he said over the sound of the rain. "I can't see anything out there."

Boggs shut off the motor and dropped a small anchor over the back to keep us from drifting into the shallows and getting stuck in the mud. Then he sat back down on the stool and folded his arms. His eyes were still cold and empty. Ellis fell into one of the lawnchairs and wiped his face and hair with a towel that he had pulled from a dry dufflebag beside the cooler. Buck and I huddled together on the deck and stared out into the gloomy swamp.

Rain drummed down on the canopy for what seemed like hours. The surface of the swamp rippled and popped like a kettle of boiling water, and we could barely see more than twenty feet away from the boat. No one said a word and soon my eyelids grew heavy. I realized that I had been up since before dawn and I was exhausted. I could feel my head drooping down to my chest, but at that point I was too tired to care. Even the loud cracks of thunder didn't startle me as I drifted off into sleep.

36

I woke up to the sound of voices.

"I think we can get started again," I heard Ellis saying.

I found myself curled up on the old tarp that had been thrown over a pile of fishing gear. I sat up, feeling a little dizzy. My jaw still ached where Ellis had hit me. I looked around and noticed the rain was starting to let up. Ellis stood at the front of the boat again, scanning the river, and Boggs was still sitting on the stool where he had been when I fell asleep.

I glanced over at Buck, who rubbed his eyes and looked around. "Where are we?" Then he turned to me. "How long was I asleep?"

I looked at my watch. It was nearly ten o'clock. "Almost an hour."

Boggs started the motor and Ellis went to the back of the boat to pull up the anchor. He tugged at the rope but it looked as if the anchor had gotten snagged on a root or something along the bottom. He scowled and leaned over to get a better grip.

As he did, a huge, black shape burst up out of the river! All I could see was a great surge of water and a flash of yellow teeth. Like the river itself had reached up to pull him under. Ellis swore and jumped backward, letting go of the rope just in time to keep his arm from being bitten off. The massive jaws slammed shut on empty air with a loud *pop*, and just as suddenly as it had appeared, the crocodile had vanished underneath the water again.

My heart pounded as Buck and I scrambled to our feet. We peeked over the side and glimpsed a huge shadow under the surface, weaving slowly side to side. It swept along the length of the boat and then slowly circled around us.

Ellis seemed to gather his wits. "It's like he was just waiting there to attack me!"

The crocodile broke the surface again, and glided back toward us. Its jagged, ridged back thumped against the side of the pontoon, giving us a good jolt. Through a flash of lightning, it open its jaws and issue a deep, growling hiss.

Ellis picked up his rifle and checked the dart he had loaded earlier. He peered through the scope and muttered to himself. Taking careful aim, he swept the barrel sideways, following the movement of his target.

He fired, peered into the water, and swore loudly. He quickly loaded another dart, took aim and fired again. And swore again.

Meanwhile, the crocodile continued circling the boat. Ellis ran to the front, loading a third dart. He took aim and fired once more as the croc came into view. A moment later, he was grinning and shaking his fist.

"I got him!" he shouted, looking back at us. "I got him that time!"

He scanned the river as the croc swept around the other side of the boat, heading back in the direction we had just come. I leaned over the rail and watched as it swam past. Through the rain, I could just make out the animal's massive shape and the bright yellow dart zipping through the water.

"Bring us around," Ellis shouted to Boggs. "Don't let him get out of sight!"

Boggs pushed the throttle forward and spun the wheel. The whole front end of the boat swung back around as we headed after the crocodile. Ellis stood at the front of the deck, his gaze fixed on the water.

With Ellis pointing and guiding, Boggs brought the boat alongside a thick patch of weeds. Through the cattails, I could see a large black shape, like a fallen tree, lying in the mud. The massive croc lay motionless with its jaws parted slightly, and its sides moving in and out. Cold, yellow eyes gazed up at us with an icy stare.

Ellis set the rifle down and brought over the big coil of rope that Finney had used on their first try. He tied another loop in the end and prepared to lower it over the side to tie up the croc's jaws. I remembered what Ellis had told us at the festival. The bite of a crocodile was extremely powerful, but its jaws weren't nearly as strong when opening. So the first thing to do would be to tie the croc's mouth shut. After that was done, it would just be a matter of securing its legs and then towing the giant lizard upriver.

Just as Ellis slipped the loop over the croc's snout, the animal clamped onto the rope and twisted sideways. The rope tore loose from Ellis's hands—nearly taking him along with it!

The croc whipped its thick tail into the air as it rolled and twisted, slamming against the pontoon several times. Ellis regained his balance and reached for the tranquilizer gun.

He groped blindly for a moment and turned to see where he'd left it. Behind him, Morris Boggs stood with the gun clutched in his beefy hands. I had been so focused on the crocodile that I never even saw him pick it up. He smashed the butt squarely into Ellis's jaw—just as Ellis had done to him earlier. Ellis reeled back against the railing and with surprising quickness, Boggs lunged forward and heaved him over the side! Ellis had barely enough time to cry out before he disappeared into the murky water, right where the crocodile was still rolling and thrashing in a blind fury.

"*That was for Max*!" Boggs shouted over the railing. With that, he climbed back behind the wheel and slammed the throttle forward. The boat lurched ahead with a roar, knocking me and Buck to the deck. We skidded backward across the rain-soaked carpet.

I grabbed the railing and Buck managed to grab hold of me. Boggs clutched the wheel, staring straight ahead.

The deck bounced and shook so hard, I thought we were going to fly right off. I couldn't believe what had just happened. Ellis was gone—probably torn to pieces by now. I looked back, straining to catch a glimpse of him or the crocodile, but all I could see was a blur of dark silhouettes in the fog.

And then I saw it…

A hand clung, white-knuckled, to the back railing. A moment later, a second hand appeared and grabbed hold as well. Next, I saw a face rising up from the back of the boat. It was Ellis Woods, his features contorted in a mad grimace as he struggled to pull himself back onto the deck.

I glanced up at Boggs who was still staring straight ahead, oblivious to everything else. The motor roared and the canopy flapped and hummed as the wind gusted over the deck, blowing paper and wrappers past us. And through all that, Ellis managed to pull himself back onto the deck without Boggs even noticing him.

His eyes held a wild look, like I had never seen before. His expression twisted into a snarl and he lunged at Boggs from behind. Boggs glanced backward, as Buck and I scrambled out of the way and then he caught sight of Ellis.

He spun around, but it was too late. Ellis plowed into him, clamping his hands around the big man's throat. Both of them fell back against the throttle, pinning it all the way forward. The boat lurched ahead as the motor raced on at top speed. The force knocked them backward onto the deck, nearly landing on top of us. The boat bounced so violently, I couldn't even move. And what was worse, I realized no one was steering!

The two men rolled across the deck, clawing, punching, and pounding each other while we sped on out of control.

At one point we hit something in the water and I felt myself flying into the air. My stomach jumped into my throat for a second and then I crashed back to the deck, landing in a pile of fishing equipment. My ribs smashed against something sharp, knocking the wind out of me.

The jolt also knocked both men apart. Ellis fell forward on top of his dufflebag while Boggs tumbled backward, nearly crushing Buck.

Boggs recovered first and grabbed the tranquilizer gun laying on the deck beside his stool. He straightened up, raising the rifle over his head like an axe as Ellis fumbled with his duffle bag.

Ellis rolled back over to face him and I heard a muffled *pop* over the sound of the engine and the wind.

Boggs dropped the rifle and looked down at his chest. A small, cherry-red stain appeared on his shirt, spreading quickly outward.

Ellis held a revolver in his grasp.

There was a moment in time where everything just seemed to stop. For that moment, I don't remember hearing the roar of the motor or the howling of the wind, and I had forgotten all about the fact that we were still racing along, out of control. I only remember Morris Boggs slumping backward in a heap right in front of Buck. Buck's face went pale as he stared down at the crumpled, bloodstained body in front of him.

Then everything snapped back on. The motor roared and the wind screamed in my ears even louder than before. I watched Ellis stumble drunkenly to the controls. He pulled himself upright and tugged back on the throttle but it wouldn't budge. He grabbed the wheel, and looked out at the river…

And for the first time since I had met him, Ellis Woods looked afraid.

37

He turned to us and shouted. "*Hold on*!"

I caught a glimpse of a large, jagged object jutting out of the water directly in our path. We slammed into it with a crunch of metal, and I felt my body sailing, head-over-heels, through the air. My limbs flailed helplessly as the world zipped past me in a blur—the deck, the sky, the trees, and then nothing but the black surface of the swamp, rushing up to meet me.

I hit the water with a thud. The impact forced the air out of my lungs and blasted water up my nose. I surfaced again, coughing and choking and gasping for breath. As I floundered in the murky water, I realized I couldn't touch the bottom.

Through the rain, I saw the wreckage of the pontoon boat, sticking up out of the water about twenty feet away. The canopy had collapsed and the deck had buckled and cracked in the middle. The back corner of the boat was propped up on the huge, gnarled tree-stump.

"Buck!" I searched through the debris but I couldn't see him anywhere. The plastic cooler bobbed in the water nearby. I grabbed hold of it and started paddling back to the boat when I spotted Buck, floating facedown in the water.

"*Buck*!" I gasped. I tugged his shirt and carefully turned him over.

Hanging onto the cooler with one arm, I put my other one around Buck's back to keep his head out of the water. I never noticed before how thin he was. His face was as white as a sheet and I couldn't tell if he was breathing or not. The sight of him so still and white made me feel sick inside. I listened for his breath and could hear a very soft, shallow wheezing sound.

"Buck," I sobbed, shaking him. "Wake up!"

He started to cough and a wave of relief swept over me when he opened his eyes. He shivered and gasped for breath and I could see a big, purple bruise on his forehead.

He looked around. "What happened?"

"I don't know," I said. "We hit a stump in the water."

Then I heard another voice. "Jake. Buck. Are you boys alright?"

It was Ellis Woods, standing on the broken deck of his boat, clutching the rail to keep himself from sliding into the water.

"I… I think we're okay," I called back.

He waved us toward him. "C'mon, you have to get out of the water."

"Everything's gonna be okay, Buck," I whispered. "We just gotta get back to the boat."

Buck started squirming and kicking. "*No!*" His eyes were round. "He—he killed Boggs… he sh-shot him!"

The image of Morris Boggs crumpling to the deck, flashed back into my head. His lifeless body must have been thrown into the water when we crashed, and was now somewhere at the bottom of the swamp. I looked from Buck to Ellis and back to Buck again. I didn't know what to do. Ellis had all but kidnapped us and now we were swimming right back toward him again! I stopped paddling toward the boat.

"Come on," Ellis said. "Hurry up!"

Buck wriggled out of my grasp and grabbed hold of the cooler for himself. He pointed a pale, shaky finger at Ellis. "You killed Boggs! You shot him!"

Ellis straightened up with a surprised look on his face. "What?" Then his expression grew cross. "He was trying to kill *me*! I was defending myself."

Buck and I glanced at each other and I don't think either of us felt certain of what to do at that point.

"What do you think he would've done with you two if I wouldn't have climbed back on board?" Ellis went on. "Don't forget, *they* were the ones who wanted to kill you boys—not me. If I wouldn't have shot Boggs, he would've killed you both by now! I saved your lives! Now come on out of that water before you—"

He never finished his sentence.

A huge black shape burst up out of the water and right onto the deck! It was Goliath. Its jaws opened and it let out a long, rolling growl. Ellis stumbled backward and the whole boat shifted under the weight of the giant lizard. Its jaws slammed shut with a loud *pop* as Ellis scrambled up the deck. He reached for the railing but lost his footing on the rain-soaked carpet and started to slide back down.

The croc planted its forelegs firmly on the front of the deck and opened its jaws again as Ellis slid closer. I could see him struggling to push himself back up the deck, but he had nothing to hang on to and nothing to stop himself. The beast lunged at him again and this time its jaws clamped down on his foot. Ellis screamed, and his voice echoed through the trees.

With a twist of its head, the croc yanked him down like a rag-doll. It loosed its grip on his ankle and bit down again across his thigh for a better hold. Ellis let out another bloodchilling cry as the crocodile's teeth sunk deep into his flesh. He looked no bigger than a child in its jaws. Kicking with his one free leg and pounding his fists on the croc's snout, he tried desperately to pry himself loose. But the huge lizard backed slowly off the wrecked boat and pulled Ellis, screaming and flailing, down into the water. His cries ended abruptly as the foamy water closed over his head.

The water churned and frothed for a long while as the crocodile rolled over and over. We caught only brief glimpses of the animal's pale belly and thick tail whipping through the water. After several moments, it all grew calm again, with only the raindrops stirring up the surface.

And that was the last time we ever saw Ellis Woods.

38

Buck and I watched in horror, unable to do anything, and I suddenly realized that we were now completely alone. Ellis, Finney and Boggs were all dead and as the churning water subsided, a terrifying thought struck me. We were going to be next!

It was as if that same thought had occurred to Buck because we both began kicking as hard as we could. I didn't know where we were headed, but I knew we had to get as far away from that wrecked boat as we could. I peered throught the rain and mist to find the shoreline but I couldn't see any sign of land anywhere. It was as if the swamp had stretched itself out in every direction and wasn't going to allow us to escape.

No matter how hard we kicked, we couldn't seem to move fast enough. The crocodile was sure to hear our splashing and would be after us in an instant. I glanced around but I couldn't find any place to hide and nothing to climb onto. I had never before felt so alone and unprotected and in desperation I did the only thing left that I could think to do.

"God, please help us!" I whispered. "*Please* help us. I'm sorry I didn't listen. I'm sorry I came out here—*please* help us!"

Then I spotted a dim shadow rising up on the surface of the river. The boat-house!

But it was still a good twenty or thirty yards away. "Kick," I said to Buck. "Kick as fast as you can!"

I looked back and didn't see anything moving on the river, though the rain made it hard to be sure. My legs ached and my muscles started cramping up, but just the thought of that creature lurking somewhere under the water made me kick harder. I wished I was just having another nightmare and any second now, I'd wake up safe at home.

We reached the boathouse and I was so exhausted I barely had enough strength to pull myself onto the dock. I collapsed and lay there, gasping for breath. My head still throbbed from where Ellis had hit me, and for a moment I thought I was going to pass out. Then I heard Buck's shaky voice.

"Jake, help me up!"

My eyes snapped open and I leaned over the edge of the dock. Buck was still in the water, looking up at me with his face all pale and his eyes wide and full of fear.

"Pull me up," he said. "My feet are stuck in the mud!"

I grabbed hold of his hands and he felt heavier than before. It was as if someone was holding on to him underneath the water and we were playing tug o' war. I got onto my knees and pulled again, as hard as I could. I felt him slowly come up out of the mud but my muscles burned so badly I had to pause and catch my breath. I scanned the river for any sign of the crocodile.

I spotted a wave on the surface no more than fifty feet away and it looked as though it was moving toward us. A sick feeling rose up inside me and I felt my eyes widen.

Buck saw my expression and turned as white as a ghost. "What is it?" He tried to look back over his shoulder. "What d'you see?"

I blinked and shook my head. "C'mon, get outta the water!" I grabbed his shoulders and pulled as hard as I could.

I could feel his body slowly rising out of the water and finally dragged him up onto the dock with me. He curled his legs up and rolled off to the side just as the great surge of water passed underneath us.

We lay there, panting and gasping for breath. We had made it. I could still see the wreckage of the pontoon boat silhouetted in the mist. I would never forget the sight of Ellis in the jaws of that crocodile. I closed my eyes and shuddered.

"What were we going to do now?" I heard Buck say.

The crocodile was still loose, and if it could kill a man like Ellis Woods as easily as it had, what chance did we have? I rolled over and scanned the water again but I couldn't see any sign of the croc. The rain had let up and the sky had begun to brighten. Abe's boat was still tied up at the dock with Buck's rifle in the bow.

All I wanted to do now was get as far away from this place as I could. I had lost. It was that simple. I thought I could kill that beast, but when I finally came face to face with it, I was overwhelmed and I knew I couldn't win.

I glanced down at Buck. His eyes were closed and he looked exhausted. I just wanted to go home and get into some dry…

Home?

I felt sick again. Ma probably had Rooster and half the town out searching for us. I pictured the look she would have on her face. She would be furious. I guess I had known all along that I was going to get in big trouble but I had also counted on bringing back the dead crocodile like some kind of trophy. That was the only thing that had made the thought of Ma's punishment seem worth while. But now I was going to have to go home empty-handed.

We got up to leave. Buck climbed into the boat and I paused to look back at the swamp. The rain had stopped and the whole place had become calm again.

Suddenly, the end of the dock exploded as the crocodile's massive head shot up from underneath the planks. It crashed through the soft wood with one mighty thrust. The whole dock jolted loose from its supports and dropped out from under my feet.

"*Buck*!" I cried out as I tumbled backwards.

The end of the dock fell into the water, and I slid down the planks as the croc emerged through the debris. The wood sank beneath its weight as it tried to climb up onto the pier.

I could see the huge lizard staring at me with cold, yellow eyes. Its jaws opened and I caught the rotting stench of its breath as it hissed. It lunged forward, snapping at my feet.

I dug my fingers into the boards and scrambled out of its way. I could only think about how I had just watched this same thing happen to Ellis Woods. At that moment, I knew I was going to die.

"Grab my hand!"

I looked up to see Buck stretched out on the level part of the dock, reaching out for me.

"Grab my hand!" he shouted again.

I reached up and felt Buck's hand close around mine. I don't know where he got the surge of strength, but he managed to pull me up onto the dock, and we clambered into the boat as the crocodile clawed its way up the planks. The wood creaked and groaned beneath its weight.

Buck struggled to untie the rope. His fingers trembled as he yanked at the knot. The rope came loose and we pushed away from the dock just as the giant lizard reached us. Its jaws slammed shut once more on empty air.

We drifted away, fumbling for the oars as the croc hissed and growled. Its jaws parted in an angry scowl.

"The gun," I cried. "Get your gun! Shoot it!"

Buck scrambled for the rifle as I rowed us further away from the dock.

We could hear a long, low creaking sound as the whole boat house leaned slowly to one side. Buck raised the rifle and took aim but the dock gave away and the crocodile plunged into the water. The boat house leaned further and finally it too collapsed like a house of cards. Within a few seconds, there was nothing left but a pile of rotted planks and moss-covered posts sticking out of the river.

Buck leaned over the bow with the rifle. “Do you see it anywhere?”

I shook my head and peered into the water. “No… I don’t—”

I choked my words off with a yelp as something rammed the bottom of the boat. The wood cracked and shuddered as the whole front tipped up out of the water. Buck dropped the rifle into the river and we both tumbled backward.

The bow splashed back down and I caught a glimpse of the crocodile moving beneath us. The hard ridges on its back scraped against the bottom of the boat.

Then the boat rose up again, tipping to one side and we fought to lean back the other way. But it was too late. Dark water rushed in over the side and wrapped around us, pulling the whole boat steadily down.

Buck and I looked at each other in silent terror. We were swamped, nearly up to our waists in the water. I could see the croc’s massive, ridged back make a wide arch and head back toward us. As it drew close, it submerged, disappearing from view.

I searched frantically for something to protect myself but the boat was sinking too fast, and I knew at any moment, those massive jaws would burst out of the water and drag me under just like it had done to Max Finney and Ellis Woods…

And to Pa.

Silence surrounded us as we peered into the murky, black water, waiting to die.

Then I spotted something out of the corner of my eye. Off toward the shore a brown, hazy shape splashed furiously.

Mo!

The old dog had come out of nowhere. He jumped into the river and bounded through the water toward us. His teeth were bared and his eyes were wild, like I had never seen before.

A great surge of water rushed over me, as the crocodile swooshed past. Its massive tail swept to the side, brushing against my chest. It felt as solid as a tree trunk and seemed to go on forever. The croc had turned away from us and now was headed for Mo!

All we could do was watch. The old dog stood up to his shoulders in the water, growling and barking so fiercely that he seemed like a different beast altogether. I had never seen him so wild before, or so vicious…

Or so alive.

He disappeared in an explosion of water and limbs. His barking ended abruptly with the fiery roar of his last, glorious attack. Through the splashing and commotion, I could see the pale belly of the croc rolling and twisting in blind fury, and the briefest glimpse of Mo's soaked body, tossing in the waves.

But all we could do was watch.

The battle ended with the thunder of a shotgun blast that echoed through the trees and rumbled off into the distance. As the churning water subsided and the smoke dissolved, I could see Abraham standing in the river, the gun frozen in his grasp and the crocodile's pale, upturned bulk floating at his feet.

It was over.

Buck and I waded numbly to shore. I couldn't bring myself to even look at the body of the crocodile as we passed it. After everything we had been through that day, part of me wanted to make sure the beast was finally dead. But I didn't want to see what it had done to Mo. I couldn't bear to see the old dog's broken body floating in the water. The last time I had seen him was when I had slammed my fist across his head. I could still see the confused expression with his ears back and his eye twitching where I had hit him.

I'll remember that look as long as I live.

Abraham didn't say a word. It was almost as if he didn't even notice we were there. He just stood in the river, staring down at the carcass of the crocodile. Then he knelt down and gently lifted the limp body of his dog from the water. I turned away, and for the first time in my life, I saw Buck Miller cry.

Abraham cradled Mo in his arms.

"I'm gonna bring him back," he said, softly. "I gotta give him a decent burial."

The three of us walked back in silence that morning. I wanted to talk to Abraham, to tell him how sorry I was and how badly I felt, but everything I wanted to say just sounded dumb and selfish to me. I wanted him to scold us or yell but he was just silent. His eyes were tired and sad. We had stolen his boat and betrayed his trust. Worst of all was that we had cost him the life of his closest and dearest companion.

I knew things would never be the same between the three of us. But as we trudged through the woods, my thoughts were drawn to Abraham and how, if he'd ever get lost in the swamp again, he wouldn't have old Mo along to help him find the way back.

39

When we finally made it back to Abe's cabin, we saw several vehicles parked in the clearing. Rooster Mason stood on Abe's front porch talking with Ma. Billy Ray and Earl Miller were also there, along with Frank Bussie and a few other folks from town. For the most part they all seemed relieved to see us but they also looked pretty upset at the same time.

Ma ran up to me and grabbed me by the shoulders. Her face was very stern and her eyes were red but she didn't cry. She just shook her head like she wanted to say something but she couldn't quite figure out how to put it into words.

"Why?" was all she managed to say.

I just looked down at my feet. It would've taken me an hour to tell her all the reasons I thought I'd had for going out there, but none of them sounded very good any more. Then I felt an ache growing deep inside my chest, and before I knew what was happening, my eyes flooded with tears.

I felt Ma pull me close to her but I couldn't stop myself from crying. I just stood there, sobbing into her shoulder in front of everybody. I could smell her shirt and her hair, and they smelled so familiar to me. A thousand memories rushed back into my head at that moment. Memories of Ma and Pa and Molly and me together, of picnics and softball games and summer vacations. Memories of back when we had been a family.

I began to cry even harder when I thought how things would never be the same now that Pa was gone, and I suddenly realized how badly I missed him. I cried when I thought about how long it had been since Ma had hugged me like that, and how long it had been since I let her. I cried because of the things I had said to her and the way I had treated her and Molly. They were trying to be a family to me but I just kept pushing them farther and farther away.

I cried because it felt so good to me then, smelling her hair and feeling her arms around me, and knowing that she would forgive me. I knew then that I still belonged and that we were still a family. Most of all, I cried when I thought of how good that made me feel, and how good it was to be back.

"I'm sorry."

"I love you, Jake," Ma whispered in my ear. "You had me so scared."

Earl Miller didn't look happy or relieved at all. He grabbed Buck by the back of the neck.

"You see what you done?" he growled. "Half the town's been out looking for you and makin' me look like a fool! Whutchyou got to say for yourself? Huh?"

But Buck didn't say a word. He wasn't crying anymore, either. He just stared straight ahead with the same look he'd had in Frank Bussie's car the night Pa had gotten killed.

Rooster had a thousand questions so Buck and I had to explain everything that had happened to us that morning. Abe stood off a little ways by himself, and afterward, Ma went over to him.

"Thank you for saving my son," she said.

Abe just nodded. "Yes ma'am."

No one else said anything to him though, at least not directly to him.

Later that day, Rooster got some men together and went back into the swamp. They found the dead crocodile and the pontoon boat just like we had said. They also found Morris Boggs' body and what was left of Ellis Woods. They never did find Max Finney, though. Not to this day.

They brought the crocodile's carcass back into town that evening and folks crowded around to see it. They were all pretty amazed and some of them even told me they were sorry for not believing me. A reporter from Chase came down to take pictures, and Buck and I got our names in the paper. We became local celebrities for a couple weeks. The article didn't mention anything about Abe though, or how he had saved our lives.

Later, some fellow from a big museum down in Florida offered the town a good deal of money for the crocodile's body. He took it back with him and stuffed it and put it on display. I heard it was a real nice exhibit but we've never gone down to see it. The town council voted to take some of the money he gave us and put up a little monument in the park for Pa and Sarah Mae Hatcher.

Up in Bilford, they closed down *GatorWorld* and auctioned everything off. It turned out that Ellis Woods had been wanted for some illegal things he'd done in Australia, which was probably why he had come here in the first place. I couldn't help feeling a little sorry for him though. He never really got to have the park he had always dreamed of, and he ended up getting killed by the same crocodile he hoped would make him rich.

Abraham buried Mo out in back of his cabin. He planted some flowers and carved a little plaque to mark the grave. It read simply: *Always Faithful.*

"Folks could stand to be a little more like dogs in some ways," Abe told me once.

I had been right about old Abe. Things never were the same between us. His boat was lying cracked and sunken at the bottom of the swamp and he had no regular way of getting into town anymore. So Ma talked the matter over with Sam Watson and Sam put it to the rest of the folks at church to pitch in and buy Abe a new boat. Of course, part of my punishment was having to do some painting and cleaning around the church and other folks' houses until I had paid at least half the cost of the boat myself.

Abe wasn't very keen on the idea, though. He said that he wanted to work off the price somehow. Ma suggested that we could use some help around our place now that Pa was gone. So Abe agreed to come into town once or twice a week and fix whatever needed to be done around the house. That raised a lot of eyebrows and gave folks quite a bit to talk about. But Ma didn't seem to care.

Buck's folks stopped letting him come over to our place as much after that and I think it was because Abe would be over so often. I don't think they ever felt grateful to Abe for what he had done. Some folks don't seem to ever change their opinions no matter what they see or learn.

I think Buck's folks—like a lot of folks in Silas—had just plain decided not to like Abe Garner a long time ago.

I remembered what Abe had said about hate and how it gets to be comfortable after a while, and how a body could grow so used to it that they wouldn't remember feeling any other way. I didn't really understand what he meant at the time, probably because I had gotten so comfortable in my own hate. But now it seemed clear to me.

Buck and I started to spend less time together after that summer. I tried to visit him on occasion but his mother would usually say he couldn't come out or that he wasn't feeling well. Sometimes I'd see him in town and we'd get a chance to talk, but it seemed like we didn't have much to say to each other anymore. Whenever I'd bring up what had happened to us in the swamp he would change the subject or make some kind of joke about it.

I think that's what hurt the most; the fact that Buck and I weren't as good of friends anymore. I could see him starting to act more and more like his father. Of course, Buck would get furious whenever I would tell him that.

I could never figure out how a fellow who disliked his own father so much could end up being so much like him. But I guess that was just another part of what hate could do to a person, and it was one of the hardest lessons I had to learn that summer ten years ago.

40

As I sat in Abe's room, paging through the old Bible, one passage in particular caught my eye.

"*For ye see your calling, brethren, how that not many wise men after the flesh, not many mighty, not many noble are called. But God hath chosen the foolish things of the world to confound the wise; and God hath chosen the weak things of the world to confound the things which are mighty; and the base things of the world and things which are despised, hath God chosen, yea, and things which are not, to bring to naught the things that are: That no flesh should glory in his presence.*"

I leaned back in the chair and rubbed my eyes. That summer seemed so long ago now, and yet reliving those events began rousing emotions I had felt so intensely then. Emotions I had since begun to tuck away deep inside, buried beneath my growing desire to get away from this little town once and for all.

I rarely thought about my father's death anymore, or how big a hole his absence had left in my life. And

Abe's part in it all had begun to fade as well. Perhaps, I was letting it. Perhaps, I didn't wish to think about how much he sacrificed, or how much I owed him.

The amber stripes of sunlight that had been draped across his bed, had now turned red-orange and shone against the far wall.

I closed the Bible and stood up to leave. Abe was fast asleep and I could hear his slow, steady breathing.

"I'll come back tomorrow," I whispered, closing the door behind me.

As I headed home that evening, I stopped at an intersection on my way through town. It was there that something caught my eye. A small shop with a neon sign in the window that read simply: *Antiques*.

Beneath the glow of the sign stood a small, hand-carved wooden figure of a dog, head tilted and ears perked forward. It didn't register with me at first, but as I waited for the light to turn green it suddenly dawned on me.

I pulled over and went inside.

A bell jingled as I entered the cluttered little shop. Old tables, chairs, nightstands, vases, bookshelves and armoires took up nearly every square foot of space. A great assortment of antique clocks, paintings and dishes hung on the walls. And in every open space on every table, and on every chest and shelf was a wooden figurine of some sort. Horses, cows, ducks, dogs, eagles, swans and people of all shapes and sizes. The place smelled like an attic and seemed to be alive with the clicking and ticking of the hundreds of clocks.

"Hello," I called.

A short, plump man came out from the back room. He was balding and doughy, with a pair of wire-rimmed glasses perched at the end of his nose. He wore an apron and smelled as if he'd been varnishing some old piece of furniture.

"Yes?" he said. "How can I help you."

I smiled. It was just as I had suspected. "Hello Mr. Haley," I said. "You probably don't recognize me."

He looked at me over his glasses and shook his head. "No…"

"My name's Jake Kelly. I met you once when you came to visit Abe Garner out at his cabin. It's been about ten years ago now."

Clarence Haley stepped a little closer and pushed his glasses up. His forehead knotted as he studied me for a second. Then his whole face seemed to brighten.

"Oohh, yes," he nodded and smiled. "I remember now. It was you and another young fellow. I remembered thinking how strange it was for Abe to have visitors—other than me of course. Yes, how are you?"

I shrugged. "Oh, I'm fine. I just came from visiting Abe at the nursing home."

Clarence clicked his tongue and shook his head. "Mmm, I went to see him yesterday. He's not doing very well they say. The doctors said it was some sort of a stroke."

I nodded. "That's what my mother said. But he seemed to recognize me okay."

"That's always a good sign." Clarence wiped his hands on his apron. "So what can I do for you, Jake?"

"Well, I was on my way home and I saw your store. I remembered you used to buy Abe's wood carvings from him and sell them here."

Clarence nodded and grinned. "Best kept secret in Chase County. In fact these are the last batch of things he was working on." He waved his hand about the room. "I just got done putting them out. I'm getting ready for a big sale tomorrow."

I went over to the window and picked up the dog that had caught my attention. Its sad eyes stared up at me mournfully. It was beautiful.

Clarence nodded, as if he knew what I was thinking. "He does good work."

"Yes he does."

"Hey," Clarence said, glancing around the room as if he was about to tell me some great secret and wanted to be sure no one else was listening. Then he leaned close and said softly, "You want to see something *real* special?"

"Sure."

He went into the back room and came out a few moments later carrying an object wrapped in a brown blanket. He set it on the counter and carefully unwrapped it. I took one look and let out a long whistle.

It was a large, wooden platter with an intricate scene carved on the interior. A crowd of people gathered around one man standing on a hill and looked to be talking to them. I could tell by the way the people were dressed that it was a scene from out of the Bible. Across the bottom ledge was the phrase: *"Blessed are the Meek"*

The detail and workmanship were the finest I had ever seen.

Clarence just smiled. "It's something ain't it?"

"It sure is," I said.

"It's a relief carving of the Sermon on the Mount," he went on. "This was Abe's last piece he was working on. Cyrus Meade commissioned it himself."

I raised my eyebrows. "Cyrus Meade?"

Clarence chuckled. "Yep, Ol' Cyrus came up with the idea himself and told me exactly what he wanted. 'Money's no object!' he said, 'I want to put it right on my mantle where everyone can see it!' So I had Abe start to work on it a few months ago and it's turned out to be his finest piece yet. Old Cyrus is paying over a thousand dollars for it too! Only thing is, he don't know it was Abe Garner that made it. I s'pect he'd have a heart attack if he ever found out it was made by a colored fella—let alone old Abe." He laughed again, even harder. "In fact, the Meades have bought more of Abe's carvings than anyone else over the years."

"I don't get it," I said.

"Well," Clarence began. "It seems Mrs. Meade fancies herself a bit an art collector. I remember the first time she came into my store. It was shortly after I had started selling Abe's woodcarvings. Well, she took one look at a pony that he had done and just fell in love with it. Said she just *had* to have it! She brought it to one of her art collector friends and they said it was some of the finest work they'd ever seen. They told her it'd be worth investing in, and well, she's been buying them ever since. She still comes in regularly once or twice a month to see what new pieces I've got."

"And they have no idea that Abe's the one who's been carving them all this time?" I started to chuckle.

Clarence nodded. "I was over at their house for a charity banquet last Christmas, and I swear, I couldn't find a single table or window sill or mantle in the whole place that didn't have something of Abe's settin' on it!"

I just shook my head and laughed.

"And the Meades of all people," Clarence laughed again. Then he paused for a moment and stared off into space as his face grew solemn. "You see, Abe used to work for Cyrus, years back."

I nodded. "Yeah, he told me about that once."

Clarence wrapped the wooden platter back up in its blanket. "He probably didn't tell you how angry Cyrus got when Abe quit and started working for himself."

I frowned. "No."

Clarence's lips grew tight. "Well, Cyrus Meade—" he paused and shook his head. "Well, let's just say he ain't a man to be crossed. Most folks don't really know what he can be like. But I've seen that side of him—the *mean* side. He's got a vicious temper—downright *vicious*! After Abe left, old Cyrus made life pretty difficult for him."

Things started to make sense to me now. Abe had told us about how he and his wife had been attacked and how their house had been burned down. Now it was making sense.

"You mean it was Cyrus Meade that burned down Abe's house?"

"I know he was behind it," Clarence said. "He's a powerful man. Folks don't just up and quit on him. Especially colored folks!"

I couldn't believe what I was hearing. "Why didn't anyone do anything about it?"

"I told you," Clarence laughed, uneasily. "Cyrus Meade's a powerful man. You don't just go and accuse him of things. You don't just go and arrest him. He's got the law here in Chase right in his hip pocket. Rooster learned that lesson the hard way when he was just a deputy. You don't just go and cross old Cyrus, no sir!"

I was getting frustrated. “So that’s it? Nobody’ll stand up to that old man just because he’s got more money’n everyone else?”

“Oh I wouldn’t say that.” Clarence smiled. “Seems to me that Abe stood up to him well enough. There’s several poor families down in Taylor’s Bend that’ve gotten clothes and shelter from the money Abe’s made over the years. He could’ve lived pretty well off with all the money he made but he chose to help out other folks who needed it more. Why, the money he got for that platter alone has gone to put a new roof on the church Abe used to go to.”

Slowly, my anger softened and I scratched my head. Clarence was right. God had worked out a beautiful sort of irony in the lives of Abe Garner and Cyrus Meade. One man had stored up treasure in heaven while the other thought he had gained the whole world but was in danger of losing his soul.

I looked around at all the bits of Abe’s handiwork. These figures had once been ordinary chunks of wood but Abe had turned them into works of art. He brought a good deal of beauty into people’s lives, even though they never knew it.

Just then, something else caught my attention. On a small table beside a rocking-chair was a chess set. I examined it closer. The pieces were carved and polished with such detail and beauty.

“Abe made this too?” I asked. An old memory came back to me. I had seen this somewhere before.

“Yessir,” Clarence nodded. “He’s made quite a few of them over the years. Why I’ve sold—”

But I was already headed for the door. “I gotta go,” I called behind me. “I just remembered something!”

41

The sun had set by the time I pulled up to Buckman's Drugstore and the sky had deepen into purple. The lights were on inside, and I could see Clem Anderson standing in the doorway. His silhouette looked more gaunt and bent than I remembered. The others were still there as well, later than usual.

Good.

I burst through the screen door and Clem stepped aside. Jolly Meyer looked startled. Mort Krasky turned and scowled at me over his glasses. Then his eyebrows went up.

"Are my eyes playing tricks on me, or is that Jacob Kelly back in town after so long?"

Yancey got up from his stool at the counter and gave me a warm handshake. "Nice to see you again, son. Mrs. Buckman mentioned you were back. You going to be staying a while or just for a visit?"

"Just a short visit, I'm afraid." I shook hands all around. "I figured you gentlemen would be here. Thought

I'd stop in to say 'hello' and maybe watch a good game of chess."

Jolly chortled. "Well, I don't know how good it is but it's chess anyway."

I stared at Mort's chess set as I drew up to the table. I picked up one of the pieces and examined it. It was beautiful! I had watched them play with this chess set for years but I had never taken the time to notice the pieces they were using. They had been carved out of oak and hickory, and the workmanship was unmistakable. I couldn't help the grin that came over my face.

"What's so funny?" Mort's friendly demeanor quickly evaporated. He had obviously been losing again.

I shook my head but I couldn't seem to wipe the smile off my face. "Nothing. It's just that I never looked close at this chess set of yours. It's really… well, it's great workmanship."

Jolly picked up a piece and examined it as well. "You know he's right, Morty. This here's a downright fine chess set you got. What say you wager it on the game?"

"Acch!" Mort scowled again. "Quit distractin' me—all of ya!"

Jolly tossed the piece up into the air and caught it again. "How much did you pay for it?"

Mort brooded over his next move. There were far less of his pieces on the board than there were of Jolly's. "More'n you could afford!" he blustered. Jolly laughed.

"Where'd you get it?" I asked.

Mort looked up and his eyes narrowed. "Why're you bein' so nosy?"

I shrugged. "I just think it's a nice board is all."

"Chase," Mort grunted and turned back to the game. "Bought it up in Chase. Paid a good penny for it, too! You don't find craftsmanship like this no more. Not these days"

"Where up in Chase?" I persisted. "Do you remember where?"

"'Course I do!" Mort snapped. "That—er… that antique place up there. The fella sells all sorts of this stuff. I went up with Clem when he got his cane. That must be ohhh… fifteen, twenny years ago by now."

"Twenny-three," Clem barked from the doorway, without turning around.

"Twenny-three years ago," Mort echoed.

I was dumbfounded. All these years I had watched them, and they had been playing on a chess set that Abe Garner himself had made. I had all I could do to keep from laughing out loud. Then something Mort had said sunk in.

Clem Anderson's cane!

I turned back to the doorway. Clem just stood there like a statue, staring outside. My gaze traveled down to the walking-stick he was leaning on.

"You mind if I have a look at your cane?" I asked.

Clem gave me a look as if he was trying to figure me out. Then he lifted his cane for me to examine. It looked like it had been fashioned from a branch, long and knotted and smoothly polished. Then I saw the handle.

It was a majestic horse's head, nostrils flared, mane blowing back, the most unique walking-stick I had ever seen. In all the years I had watched old Clem walking around with that cane, I had never looked close enough to really see it. And now… now I saw it was beautiful.

"Wow," I breathed.

"Y'don't see work like that no more," Clem muttered. "Nowadays, everything's chopped-out and mass-produced. No one takes the time to make anything unique or special. But this here's a one-of-a-kind! Handmade!"

I smiled. "Who made it? Do you know?"

Clem frowned. "Nope. But he was good. That's all I can say. You look at that detail. That's real craftsmanship. That's a master wood-carver! Don't see work like'at no more. No sir!"

"Looks expensive," I grinned.

"Bahh!" Clem scowled and snatched the stick back. Then he glanced at his watch and turned to the others. "I'm goin' home," he muttered and marched out the door.

As I watched Clem Anderson hobbling off down the sidewalk, I realized that I had never noticed before how much he leaned on that cane.

Early the next morning, I drove back to Chase to visit Abe again. I brought the old Bible along with me because I knew he'd want me to read to him from it. I couldn't wait to tell him about what I had discovered. I knew he'd be happy to hear what everybody thought of his craftsmanship. I knew that would make his day…

I stopped at the door to his room.

A stout woman stood beside the bed, snapping a fresh pillow into a clean pillowcase. The blinds were pulled up, flooding the room with daylight, and the bed had crisp, clean sheets. I stepped back out to check the room number.

The woman turned and saw me. "Can I help you?"

"I was looking for Abe Garner," I said. "Did they move him to another room?"

She looked down for a moment and then back to me. "I'm sorry, but Mr. Garner passed away last night."

I just stood there, staring at her. It took a moment for her words to sink in, and when they did, I felt them hit me like a truck. I don't know why I was so surprised. Deep down, I knew he was going to die. I just didn't expect it to be this soon. I didn't even get a chance to tell him about his carvings and all the folks who'd bought them. I didn't get to tell him how proud I was of him. I didn't get to tell him so much of what I wanted to say.

"Oh…" I said, softly.

The woman finished making the bed, threw the rest of the sheets into a large bin and rolled it toward the doorway. "Did you know him?"

I nodded absently. "Yes, I did."

"Did you know that other fellow, too?"

I looked up. "Other fellow?"

"There was another man that come by a few minutes ago. He was asking about Mr. Garner, too. He seemed very upset, but he didn't tell me his name."

"How long ago?"

"Just a few minutes." She pointed down the hall. "He left just before you got here. He was wearin' a gray suit."

It was curiosity more than anything that caused me to go after him. I hurried down the hall and back out the front doors. I scanned the parking lot, but I couldn't see any sign of the him. It was probably no one I knew, but still, who else would come by to visit Abe Garner?

Then I saw a black man in a gray suit sitting on a bench. His hair was peppered with tinges of gray. He didn't notice me as I drew up. He just stared into the distance, but something in his face looked vaguely familiar. I took a breath and made my guess…

"Mr. Garner?"

He looked up at me and frowned.

"Are you Paul Garner?" I asked again.

"Do I know you?" His voice was soft and I could definitely see a resemblance to old Abe.

I smiled and shook my head. "No sir. But I knew your father. He… he told me about you once."

Paul Garner looked confused for a moment. Then he breathed a long sigh. "I guess I was just a few hours too late."

"I'm sorry for your loss."

There was a long pause, then Paul spoke again. "You said you knew him?"

"Yeah," I said, "I got to know him about ten years ago. He… well, he saved my life."

"What's your name?"

"Jake," I said, "Jake Kelly."

Paul's gaze fell. "Well, you want to hear something sad, Jake Kelly? You may have known my father better than I did. I haven't talked to him in over thirty years."

I looked down at the Bible in my hands. "You know, Abe gave this to me yesterday." I held it out to him. "But I think he really wanted you to have it."

Paul stared at it for a moment. I could see his eyes grow misty as he took the Bible from my hands.

"It was the only thing he really valued," I said.

Paul held the Bible gingerly and opened it up. He began to page through it and a tear rolled down his cheek. I could only guess at what he was feeling at that moment.

Sorrow? Regret? I wondered what had caused him to hate his own father for so long? Why had he lived all that time without ever speaking to him? And what made him finally decide to come back?

He had come all this way after all these years only to find that his father had just died and he'd been a few hours too late. I began to understand. And I began to pity him.

After a while, he wiped his eyes and looked up at me again. "You said he saved your life?"

I nodded and couldn't help grinning. "Yeah, about ten years ago. But it's a long story."

Paul slid over on the bench. "Well, I've got plenty of time."

Then I remembered something Abe told me once about my father's death. He said, sometimes God lets bad things happen for reasons we don't understand directly. He said there were probably a lot of reasons why God let my father get killed and that it might be a while before I understood any of them, and that I may never understand *all* of them.

As I sat down to tell Paul Garner about the kind of man his father was, I wondered if maybe this wasn't one of those reasons. I had been like all those folks who had made up their minds about old Abe without ever taking the time to learn the truth. If Pa hadn't died, I never would've come to know Abe or discovered the kind of man he truly was. And I wouldn't have been able to share that glimpse with his son.

Abraham Garner wasn't someone most folks would consider to be successful. But he was meek and kind and gentle and wise. And I am better off for having come to know him that June when I was twelve.

ABOUT THE AUTHOR:

Tom Pawlik is the highly imaginative, Christy Award-winning author of ***Vanish***, ***Valley of the Shadow***, ***Beckon***, ***The Way Back, Son of Man,*** and the novella ***Recollection*** from the ***7 Hours anthology***. His thought-provoking, edge-of-your-seat thrillers are infused with nonstop suspense that grabs you on the first page and won't let go until the last.

Tom's fascination with the weird, the creepy and the unknown began at an early age when he was introduced to a bizarre 19th century German story book called *Der Struwwelpeter*. The book was a collection of nightmarish morality tales by a German physician who obviously had too much time on his hands and no children of his own. The morbid nursery rhymes—sort of a Mother Goose meets Stephen King—included the frightful *Daumenlutscher* (Thumbsucker), a disturbing yarn about a boy who was warned that if he continued to suck his thumbs, the local tailor would chop them off with his sewing shears. Other tales warned against playing with matches and being overly messy. Needless to say, Tom never played with matches, generally kept his room clean, and to this day retains the use of both his thumbs.

But the psychological damage was already done, and Tom's warped imagination turned him to writing his own creepy stories at a rather young age. Alas, no publishers were brave enough to bring his stories to print, so Tom would not realize his life-long dream of becoming a published author until the ripe old age of forty-two. Today, Tom is happily married with six children of his own... who, oddly enough, never sucked their thumbs.

Also from **Mo Dog Media**

Frank Coswell embarks on a road trip from Chicago to Palm Springs, looking forward to an early retirement with plenty of sun and golf. But the truth is, he's running from dark secrets in his past. And when he picks up a hitchhiker along the way, he's not prepared for what happens.

This one is so good, you'll want to read it twice!

MORE NOVELS FROM TOM PAWLIK:

VANISH:

VALLEY OF THE SHADOW:

BECKON:

RECOLLECTION (7HOURS ANTHOLOGY):

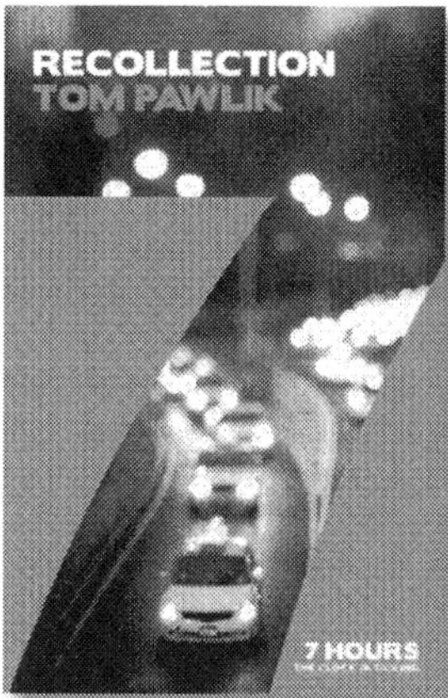

Made in the USA
Monee, IL
25 May 2022

97010234R00151